The Glass Word

The Glass Word

KAI MEYER

Translated by Elizabeth D. Crawford

MARGARET K. MCELDERRY BOOKS
NEW YORK   LONDON   TORONTO   SYDNEY

Margaret K. McElderry Books
An imprint of Simon & Schuster Children's Publishing Division
1230 Avenue of the Americas, New York, New York 10020
Published by arrangement with Loewe Verlag
First U.S. edition, 2008
Book design by Ann Zeak
The text for this book is set in Stempel Garamond.
Manufactured in the United States of America
2 4 6 8 10 9 7 5 3 1
Library of Congress Cataloging-in-Publication Data
Meyer, Kai.
[Gläserne wort]
The glass word / Kai Meyer ; translated by Elizabeth D. Crawford.—1st U.S. ed.
p. cm.—(Dark reflections ; bk. 3)
Translation of: Das gläserne wort.
Summary: While Merle, Junipa, and the great flying stone lion accompany
an Egyptian high priest to the fortress of the powerful sphinx, Serafin
and Eft voyage deep beneath the ocean to ask the help of a sea witch
in freeing Venice from the Pharoah and his mummy warriors.
ISBN-13: 978-0-689-87791-9 (hardcover)
ISBN-10: 0-689-87791-9 (hardcover)
[1. Magic—Fiction. 2. Animals, Mythical—Fiction. 3. Orphans—Fiction.
4. Mirrors—Fiction. 5. Fantasy.] I. Crawford, Elizabeth D. II. Title.
PZ7.M57171113Gla 2008
[Fic]—dc22
2006033185

Contents

1

ICE AND TEARS

THE PYRAMIDS ROSE OUT OF DEEP SNOW.

Around them stretched the Egyptian desert, buried under the mantle of a new ice age. Its sand hills were frozen stiff, its dunes piled high with drifts of snow. Instead of heat waves, ice crystals danced over the plain in swirling wind gusts that revolved a few times and feebly collapsed again.

Merle was crouching in the snow on one of the upper steps of the pyramid, with Junipa's head resting in her lap. The girl's mirror eyes were closed, the lids trembling as though behind them a few beetles were struggling to get free. Ice crystals had caught in Junipa's eyelashes and eyebrows and made them both seem even lighter. With her white skin and her smooth, pale blond hair she looked like a porcelain doll, even without the hoarfrost that was gradually covering both girls: fragile and a little sad, as if she were always thinking of a tragic loss in her past.

Merle was miserably cold: Her limbs trembled, her fingers shook, and every breath she took felt as if she were sucking ground glass into her lungs. Her head ached, but she didn't know if it was because of the cold or what she'd endured on their flight out of Hell.

A flight that had brought them straight here. To Egypt. In the desert. Where the sand and dunes were buried under a three-foot-deep layer of snow.

Junipa murmured something and frowned, but still she didn't open her eyes. Merle didn't know what would happen when Junipa finally awoke. Her friend was no longer herself since her heart had been replaced with a fragment of the Stone Light when she was in Hell. In the end Junipa had tried to turn Merle over to her enemies. The Stone Light, that incomprehensible power in the center of Hell, held her firmly in its grip.

She was still unconscious, but when she woke up . . . Merle didn't want to think about it. She'd fought with her friend once, and she wouldn't do it again. She was at the end of her strength. She didn't *want* to fight anymore, not against Junipa, not against the Lilim down below in Hell, and also not against the henchmen of the Egyptian Empire up here. Merle's courage and determination were exhausted, and she only wanted to sleep. She leaned back, relaxed, and waited for the frosty wind to rock her into an icy slumber.

"No!"

The Flowing Queen roused Merle from her stupor. The voice in her head was familiar to her and at the same time infinitely strange. As strange as the being who'd installed herself inside her and ever since had accompanied her every thought, her every step.

Merle shook herself and marshaled her last reserves. She *must* survive!

She quickly raised her head and looked up at the sky.

A bitter battle was still raging up there.

Her companion, Vermithrax, the winged lion of stone, was engaged in a daredevil air duel with one of the sunbarks of the Egyptian Empire. Vermithrax's black obsidian body had glowed ever since his bath in the Stone Light, as if someone had poured him from molten lava. Now the lion traced a glowing trail in the sky, like a shooting star.

Merle watched as Vermithrax again rammed the wobbling sunbark from above, fastened himself to the sickle-shaped aircraft, and remained sitting on top of it. His wings settled on the left and right of the fuselage, which was about three times as long as a Venetian gondola. The craft rapidly lost altitude under the lion's mighty weight, rushing toward the ground, toward the pyramid—and toward Merle and Junipa!

Merle finally snapped out of her trance. It was as if the cold had laid an armor plate of ice around her, which she now burst with a single jerk. She leaped up, seized the unconscious Junipa under the arms, and pulled her through the snow.

They were on the upper third of the pyramid. If the sunbark's crash shattered the stone, they hadn't a chance. An avalanche of stone blocks would pull them with it into the interior of the structure.

Vermithrax looked up for the first time and saw where the bark's tumbling flight was heading. The air resounded with a sharp crack as he pulled his wings apart and tried to steer the bark's descent. But the vehicle was too heavy for him. It continued on its downward course, straight toward the side of the pyramid.

Vermithrax roared Merle's name, but she didn't take the time to look up. She was pulling Junipa backward along the stone step. She had to pull her foot out of deep snow with every step, and she was in constant danger of stumbling. She knew that she wouldn't be able to stand up again once she fell down. Her strength was as good as used up.

A shrill howling pierced Merle's ears as the sunbark came nearer—an arrow point aimed at her by Fate; there was hardly any doubt that it would knock her into kingdom come.

"Junipa," she gasped out, "you have to help me. . . ."

But Junipa didn't move, though behind her closed lids there was twitching and trembling. But for those signs of life, Merle might as well have been dragging a corpse through the snow, for Junipa no longer had a heart to beat. Only stone.

"Merle!" Vermithrax roared again. "Stay where you are!"

She heard him, but she didn't react and had taken two more steps before the words got through to her.

Stay where she was? What the devil—

She looked back, saw the bark—so close!—saw Vermithrax on the fuselage with outspread wings, which the headwind was trying to blow backward, and recognized what the lion had realized a moment before she did.

The sunbark wobbled even more, swerved from its original trajectory, and was now rushing toward the opposite edge of the pyramid's side, just where Merle had been trying to get herself and Junipa to safety.

It was pointless to turn around. Instead, Merle let go of Junipa, threw herself over her, buried her face in her arms, and awaited the impact.

It took its time—two seconds, three seconds—but when the crash came, it felt as if someone had struck a gong right beside Merle's ears. The vibration was so great that she was sure the pyramid was going to collapse.

The stone was shaken a second time when Vermithrax came down beside them, more falling than landing, snatched up both girls in his paws, and carried them into the air. His body was cool, despite the glow he gave off.

His precaution turned out to be unnecessary. The pyramid was still standing. Occasional clumps of snow broke from the edges and slid one or two steps deeper, to be dispersed in blinding clouds of crystals, momentarily wrapping the incline in a fog of ice. Only after the avalanche had settled could Merle tell what had become of the bark.

The golden sickle lay on one of the upper steps, only a little beyond the place where Merle and Junipa had cowered seconds before. The vehicle had landed sideways, close to the wall of the next step up. From the air, Merle could see only a little damage, a hole in the upper side that Vermithrax had torn in the fuselage.

"Put us down again, please," said Merle to the lion, breathless certainly, but at the same time so relieved that she felt new strength streaming through her.

"Too dangerous." The lion's breath formed white clouds in the ice-cold air.

"Come on. Don't you want to know what was in the bark?"

"Absolutely not!"

"*Mummy soldiers,*" the Flowing Queen interjected in Merle's mind, inaudible to the two others. "*A whole troop of them. And a priest who held the bark in the air with his magic.*"

Merle cast a look over at Junipa, who was dangling in Vermithrax's second paw. Her lips moved.

"Junipa?"

"What's up?" asked Vermithrax.

"I think she's waking up."

"Once again, just at the right moment," the Queen bleated. *"Why do these things always happen just when one does* not *need them?"*

Merle ignored the voice inside her. No matter what it might mean for them all or whether they'd have more trouble because of it, she was glad that Junipa was coming to herself again. After all, she'd been the one who knocked Junipa unconscious, and the thought continued to pain her. But her friend had left her no choice.

"If she still is your friend." It wasn't the first time that the Flowing Queen had read her thoughts; the bad habit had begun way back.

"Of course she is!"

"You saw her. And heard what she said. Friends do not behave that way."

"That's the Stone Light. Junipa couldn't help it."

"That changes little about the fact that she may try to do you harm."

Merle didn't answer. They were floating a good ten yards over the nearest pyramid step. Gradually Vermithrax's firm grip began to hurt.

"Set us down," she asked him once more.

"At least the pyramid appears to be stable," the lion agreed.

"Does that mean we can look at the bark?"

"I didn't say that."

"But there's nothing moving down there. If there are really mummies in there, they must be—"

"Dead?" the Queen asked pointedly.

"Out of action."

"Maybe. Or maybe not."

"Those are just exactly the sort of remarks we need," said Merle caustically.

Vermithrax had made his decision. With gentle wing beats he brought Junipa and Merle back to secure ground—as secure as four-thousand-year-old pyramids situated over an entrance to Hell are.

He first set Merle down on one of the stone steps. After she was able to stand, she carefully took Junipa from Vermithrax's grasp. Junipa's lips were still moving. Weren't her eyes open a crack now? Merle thought she saw the mirror glass under the lids.

Slowly she let her friend down into the snow. She was burning to run over to the bark, but she had to take care of Junipa first.

She gently stroked Junipa's cheek. When her frozen fingers touched the skin, it was as if ice met ice. She wondered how long it would be before the first frostbite showed.

"Junipa," she whispered. "Are you awake?"

From the corner of her eye she saw Vermithrax's glowing body tense, noticed the mighty muscle cords that clenched under the obsidian-like fists. The lion was ready to respond to an attack immediately. And his distrust was directed not toward the sunbark alone. Junipa's treachery had made him just as mistrustful as the Queen, only he didn't show it so openly.

The girl's eyelids fluttered, then opened hesitantly. Merle saw her own face reflected in the mirror shards Junipa had for eyes. She hardly recognized herself. As if someone had shown her a picture of a snowman, with ice-encrusted hair and blue-white skin.

We need warmth, she thought with alarm. We'll die here outside.

"Merle," came weakly from Junipa's chapped lips. "I . . . You have . . ." Then she fell silent again and clutched the hem of Merle's dress. "It's so cold. Where . . . are we?"

"In Egypt." Although she said it herself, it seemed as absurd to Merle as if she'd said "On the moon."

Junipa stared at her with her mirror eyes, but the gleaming glass betrayed none of her thoughts. When the magic mirror maker Arcimboldo had implanted them in her and made the blind girl see, Merle had found the gaze of the mirrors cold; but the feeling had never been as appropriate as it was now, in the middle of this new ice age.

"Egypt . . ." Junipa sounded hoarse but no longer as indifferent as she had inside the pyramid, when she'd tried to talk Merle into remaining in Hell. A breath of hope rose in Merle. Had the Stone Light lost its power over Junipa up here?

From the direction of the bark came a metallic sound, followed by creaking.

With a threatening growl, Vermithrax whirled around. Again the ground trembled under his feet.

At the side of the bark—in the wall now facing skyward—a section of the metal snapped outward and stood there for a moment, trembling like an upright insect's wing.

Vermithrax pushed protectively in front of the girls, blocking Merle's view. She almost put her neck out of joint in order to see between his legs.

Something worked itself out of the opening. Not a mummy soldier. Not a priest.

"*A sphinx,*" whispered the Flowing Queen.

The creature had the upper body of a man, whose hips merged into the body of a lion, with sand-colored fur, four muscular legs, and razor-sharp wild animal claws. He appeared not to be aware of Vermithrax and the girls at all, he was so battered by the crash. Blood was flowing into his fur from several contusions; a gouge in his head was particularly deep. After several attempts, he managed to climb feebly out of the hatch, until in the end he lost his balance, rolled over the edge of the bark's fuselage, and fell. He crashed onto the next lower step, as hard as a full-grown buffalo. His blood sprinkled the snow. He lay there, unmoving.

"Is he dead?" asked Merle.

Vermithrax stamped through the snow up to the bark and looked down at the sphinx. "Looks pretty much like it."

"Do you think there are more inside?"

"I'm going to look." He approached the bark in stalking position, low to the ground and with mane on end.

"If the bark was only a scout, what was a sphinx doing on board?" asked the Queen. *"Normally a priest is available for such tasks."*

Merle didn't know too much about the hierarchy of the Egyptian Empire, but she did know that the sphinxes ordinarily occupied the most important positions. Only the high priests of Horus stood between them and Pharaoh Amenophis.

Vermithrax climbed onto the fuselage as agilely as a young cat. Only the soft scratching of his claws on the metal betrayed him. But if there were actually anyone still alive inside, their voices would have warned him long before.

"Why a sphinx?" asked the Queen once more.

"How should I know?"

Junipa's hand felt for Merle's. Their fingers closed around each other's. In spite of the tension, Merle was relieved. At least for the moment, it appeared that the

Stone Light had lost its influence over Junipa. Or its interest in her.

Vermithrax, still prowling, covered the last distance to the open hatch. He pushed his gigantic front claws to the edge of the opening, stretched his neck forward, and looked down.

The attack they were all expecting did not come.

Vermithrax walked all around each part of the hatch that was not obscured by the open cover. He looked into the interior from all sides.

"I am so cold!" Junipa's voice sounded as if she were far away in her thoughts, as if her mind had still not processed what had happened.

Merle pulled her closer, but her eyes remained fixed on Vermithrax.

"He will not go inside there," said the Queen.

What do you want to bet? Merle thought.

The obsidian lion made an abrupt leap. His powerful body just fit through the opening, and as he disappeared inside, its outline glowed. From one moment to the next, their surroundings became gray and colorless. For the first time Merle became conscious of how very much his brightness had made the icy surface around them sparkle.

She waited for a noise, the sound of battle, cries and roars and the hollow crashing of bodies banging against the bark's fuselage. But it remained quiet, *so* quiet that now she began to really worry about Vermithrax.

"Do you think something's happened to him?" she asked the Queen, but then she saw Junipa shrug her shoulders wearily because Merle had spoken the question aloud. Of course after all she'd been through, Junipa had probably forgotten what had happened to Merle. Who could really believe that the Flowing Queen—a legend, an incomprehensible power of whom the Venetians whispered reverently—would one day be living in Merle's mind?

So much had happened since then. Merle wanted nothing more than to tell Junipa of her adventures, of her journey through Hell, where they hoped to find help against the overwhelming Empire. But instead they'd found only sorrow and danger and the Stone Light waiting for them. But Junipa, too. Merle was burning to find out her story. She wanted to rest somewhere and do what she'd done with her friend before, night after night: talk with each other.

A metallic *clang* sounded from inside the bark.

"Vermithrax?"

The lion did not answer.

Merle looked at Junipa. "Can you stand up?"

A dark shadow passed over the mirror eyes. It took a moment for Merle to realize that it was only the reflection of a raptor that was flying over their heads.

"I can try," said Junipa. She sounded so weak that Merle had serious doubts.

Junipa struggled to her feet; heaven only knew where she got the strength. But then Merle remembered how the fragment of the Stone Light in Junipa's chest had healed her wounds in seconds.

Junipa stood up and dragged herself closer to the bark along with Merle.

"Do you mean to climb down there after him?" the Queen asked in alarm.

Someone has to see about him, Merle thought.

Secretly the Queen was just as worried about Vermithrax as Merle was, and she didn't conceal this feeling especially well: Merle felt the Queen's unrest as if it were her own.

Just before she reached the farthest tip of the curving fuselage she looked down at the lifeless sphinx two yards deeper in the snow. He had lost still more blood. It fanned out like an irregular red star, pointing in all directions. The blood was already beginning to freeze.

Merle looked up at the hatch again, but the fuselage of the bark was too high and they'd come too close to be able to see the opening now. It wouldn't be easy to climb up on the smooth surface.

A loud *crack* made them jump, yet it instantly resolved their fears.

Vermithrax was again perched on the fuselage. He had catapulted out of the hatch in one leap and was looking down at the girls with gentle lion eyes.

"Empty," he said.

"Empty?"

"No human, no mummy, and no priests."

"That is impossible," said the Queen in Merle's thoughts. *"The Horus priests would not allow the sphinxes to go on patrol alone. Priests and sphinxes hate each other like poison."*

You know a whole lot about them, Merle thought.

"I have protected Venice from the Empire and its powers as long as I could. Do you really wonder that I learned at least a little about them from experience?"

Vermithrax unfolded one wing and lifted first Merle, then, hesitantly, Junipa beside him on the golden fuselage of the bark. The lion pointed to the hatch. "Climb inside. It's warmer inside there. At least you won't freeze to death."

He had scarcely finished speaking when something gigantic, massive rose up from the emptiness beside the wreck and landed on the fuselage behind the girls with a wet, thumping sound. Before Merle realized it, Junipa's hand was snatched from her own.

She whirled around. Before her stood the wounded sphinx, holding Junipa in his huge hands. She looked even more fragile than before, like a toy in the claws of that beast.

She didn't scream, she only whispered Merle's name, and then she was utterly silent.

Vermithrax was about to shove Merle to one side to better get at the sphinx on the bark. But the creature shook his head, with effort, as if every movement cost him hideous pain. Blood dripped from his head wound onto Junipa's hair and froze solid.

"I'll tear the child to pieces," he got out with difficulty, in Merle's language, but with an accent that sounded as if his tongue were swollen; perhaps it actually was.

"*Say nothing.*" The voice of the Queen sounded imploring. "*Let Vermithrax deal with it.*"

But Junipa—, Merle began.

"*He knows what to do.*"

Merle's eyes fastened on Junipa's face. The girl's fear seemed to freeze on her features. Only the mirror eyes remained cold and detached.

"Don't come any nearer," said the sphinx. "She will die."

Vermithrax's lion tail thrashed slowly from one side to the other, back and forth, again and again. A shrill squeal sounded as he extended his claws and the points scratched on the fuselage.

The sphinx's situation was hopeless. In a fight he wouldn't have been able to do anything against Vermithrax. And yet he armed himself in his own way: He held Junipa in his grip and used her like a shield. Her feet were dangling twenty inches off the surface.

Merle noticed that the sphinx was not standing securely. He had bent his right foreleg just enough that the ball of the paw no longer touched the snow. He was in pain and in despair. That made him unpredictable.

Merle forgot the cold, the icy wind, even her fear.

"Nothing's going to happen to you," she said to Junipa, not certain whether her voice would reach her friend. Junipa looked as if with each breath she was pulling back into herself a little deeper.

Vermithrax took a step toward the sphinx, who evaded him, grasping his hostage tightly.

"Stay where you are," he said in a strained voice. The glow of the obsidian lion was mirrored in his eyes. He didn't understand who or what was standing there before him: a mighty winged lion, who shone like freshly wrought iron— never before had the sphinx seen such a creature.

This time Vermithrax obeyed the demand and halted. "What is your name, sphinx?" he asked in a growl.

"Simphater."

"Good, Simphater, then consider. If you harm a hair of the girl, I will kill you. You know that I can do it. So quickly that you won't even feel it. But also slowly, if you make me angry."

Simphater blinked. Blood was running into his left eye, but he hadn't a hand free to wipe it away. "Stay where you are!"

"You already said that."

Merle saw how every sinew and muscle in the sphinx's arms strained. He changed his grip, grabbed Junipa by both her upper arms, and held her out in the air.

He's going to tear her apart, she thought in a panic. He'll simply break her in two!

"*No,*" said the Queen without any real conviction.

He's going to kill her. The pain is driving him mad.

"*Sphinxes can tolerate much more pain than you humans.*"

Vermithrax radiated endless patience. "Simphater, you're a soldier, and I won't try to lie to you. You know that I can't let you go. Nevertheless, I have no interest in your death. You can fly this bark, and we want to get away from here. That's very convenient, don't you think?"

"Why the bark?" said Simphater with irritation. "We fought up there. You can fly. You don't need me."

"I don't. But the girls. A flight on my back in this cold would kill them in a few minutes."

Simphater's blurry eyes wandered over Merle and the lion, then hovered over the dazzling white of the endless snow fields. "Did *you* do that?"

Vermithrax raised an eyebrow. "What?"

"The ice. It doesn't snow in this desert . . . it never did before."

"Not we," said Vermithrax. "But we know who is responsible for it. And he is a powerful friend."

Again the sphinx blinked. He seemed to be weighing whether Vermithrax was lying to him. Was the lion just trying to make him unsure? His tail switched back and forth, and a drop of sweat appeared on his forehead, despite the icy cold.

Merle held her breath. Suddenly Simphater nodded

almost imperceptibly and set Junipa down gently. She only realized what was happening to her when her feet touched the golden surface of the bark. Stumbling, she ran over to Merle. The two embraced each other, but Merle did not go below. She wanted to look the sphinx in the eye.

Vermithrax had not moved. He and Simphater stared at each other.

"You are keeping your word?" asked the sphinx, sounding almost astonished.

"Certainly. If you get us away from here."

"And do not try any magic tricks," Merle added, but now it was the voice of the Queen who spoke out of her. "I know the sphinx magic, and I will know if you try to use it."

Simphater stared at Merle in surprise and seemed to be asking himself whether he'd underestimated the girl at the lion's side.

No one was more astonished at her words than Merle herself, but she made no attempt to deny the Queen the use of her tongue—even though she'd found out that she could do it.

"No magic," said the Queen, once more through Merle's mouth. And then she added some words to it, which belonged neither to Merle's vocabulary nor to that of any other human being. They belonged to the language of the sphinxes, and their import seemed to impress Simphater deeply. Once more he eyed Merle suspiciously, then his expression changed to one of respect. He lowered his head and bowed humbly.

"I will do what you desire," he said.

Junipa looked confused, but Vermithrax knew well who spoke from Merle. Better than any human he sensed the presence of the Queen, and Merle had asked herself more than once what constituted the bond between the spirit creature inside her and the obsidian lion.

"You get in first," he said to Simphater, pointing to the hatch.

The sphinx nodded. His paws left red impressions in the snow.

A shrill cry resounded over the icy plain, so piercing that Merle and Junipa put their hands over their ears. The scream reverberated over the landscape, out to the scattered snow pyramids in the distance. The ice crust cracked, and at the edges of the steps above and below the bark, icicles broke off and bored six feet deeper into the snow.

Merle knew that sound.

The cry of a falcon.

Simphater froze.

Over the horizon appeared the outline of a gigantic raptor, many times higher than all the pyramids, feathered in gold and with wings so huge it looked as if he intended to embrace the world. When he spread them, they triggered a raging snowstorm.

Merle watched as the icy masses of the plain were whipped and whirled up to them as a white cloud wall; just before they reached the pyramid they lost their strength and collapsed. The gigantic falcon opened his beak and again let out the high scream, still louder this time, and now all around them the snow was in motion, trembling and vibrating as if there were an earthquake. Junipa clung to Merle, and Merle instinctively clutched at Vermithrax's long mane.

Simphater lapsed into utter panic, shrank back with wide eyes, lost his balance on the smooth fuselage of the sunbark, and skittered over the edge into empty space, this time with much greater momentum than before. The next pyramid step did not stop him; he fell farther down, his long legs snapped, his head cracked several times on ice and stone, and the sphinx finally came to rest at the foot of the pyramid, many steps and yards below them, twisted so unnaturally that there could be no doubt that he was dead.

The falcon screamed for a last time, then he closed the wings in front of his body the way a magician closes his cape after a successful magic trick, hid himself behind them, and dissolved.

Moments later the horizon was empty and all was as before—with the exception of Simphater, who lay lifeless in the snow below them.

"Into the bark, quickly!" cried Vermithrax. "We must—"

"Leave?" asked someone above them.

On the next higher step stood a man, unclothed despite the cold. For a moment Merle believed she saw fine feathers on his body, but then they faded. Perhaps an illusion. His skin had once been painted golden, but now only a few smeared stripes of color were left. A fine-meshed netting of gold had been implanted in his bald scalp. It covered the entire back of his head and reached forward to his eyebrows, looking like the pattern of a chessboard.

They all recognized him again: Seth, the highest of the Horus priests of Egypt, personal confidant of the Pharaoh and second man in the hierarchy of the Empire.

He had flown out of the underworld in the form of a falcon after his failed attempt to assassinate Lord Light, the ruler of Hell. Vermithrax had followed the bird, and so they found the pyramid exit that brought them back to the surface.

"Without me you would have gotten nowhere," said Seth, and yet it didn't sound half as fear-inspiring as he probably intended.

The sight of the icy desert disconcerted him, just as it did all the others. At least he didn't appear to be freezing, and Merle saw that the snow under his feet was melting. Not without reason was Seth counted the most powerful magician among the Pharaoh's servants.

"Into the bark!" whispered Vermithrax to the girls. "Hurry up!"

Merle and Junipa rushed over to the hatch, but Seth's voice halted them again.

"I don't want to fight. Not now. And most certainly not here."

"What then?" Merle's voice trembled slightly.

Seth seemed to be considering. "Answers." His hand included the breadth of the icy plain. "To all this."

"We know nothing about it," said Vermithrax.

"You claimed something different before. Or were you trying to deceive poor Simphater in his last moments? You know who's responsible for this. You said he was your friend."

"We are not interested in a quarrel with you either, Horus priest," said Vermithrax. "But we are not your slaves."

The priest was an enemy like no other, and it was not Vermithrax's way to underestimate his opponent.

Seth smiled nastily. "You're Vermithrax, right? Whom the Venetians in ancient times called traitor. You left your folk of the talking stone lions behind in Africa a long time ago to go to war against Venice. Don't give me that thunderstruck look, lion—yes, I know you. And as for your not intending to be slaves: I have no desire to have a servant like you. Your kind is too dangerous and unpredictable. A painful experience we had to suffer with the rest of your people too. The Empire has ground their cadavers to sand in the corpse mills of Heliopolis and scattered them on the banks of the Nile."

Merle couldn't have moved, even if she'd wanted to. Her limbs were frozen; even her heart seemed to stand still. She stared at Vermithrax, saw the anger, the hatred, the despair in his glowing lava eyes. He'd been driven by the hope of one day returning to his people ever since she'd known him.

"You lie, priest," he said tonelessly.

"Maybe. Perhaps I am lying. But perhaps not."

Vermithrax crouched to spring, but the Queen called through Merle's mouth, "Don't! If he is dead, we will never get away from here alive!"

For a moment it looked as though there was nothing that could hold Vermithrax back. Seth even took a step backward. Then, however, the lion got control of himself, but he maintained his ready-to-spring stance.

"I will find out if you spoke the truth, priest. And if the answer is yes, I will find you. You and all who are responsible for it."

Seth smiled again. "Does that mean that we can now set personal feelings aside and come to the nub of our business? You tell me what is going on in Egypt—and I will take you away from here in the bark."

Vermithrax was silent, but Merle said slowly, "Agreed."

Seth winked at her, then looked again at the lion. "Have I your word, Vermithrax?"

The obsidian lion drew his front paw over the metal of

the bark. It left behind four finger-wide furrows, as deep as Merle's index finger was long. He nodded, only once and very grimly.

Ground to sand in the corpse mills, echoed again in Merle's thoughts. An entire people. *Could* that be at all true?

"*Yes,*" said the Queen. "*This is the Empire. Seth is the Empire.*"

Maybe he's lying, she thought.

"*Who knows?*"

But you don't believe it?

"*Vermithrax will find out the truth sometime. What I believe is unimportant.*"

Merle wanted to go to Vermithrax and embrace his powerful neck, reassure him, and weep with him. But the lion stood there as if turned to ice.

She motioned to Junipa and climbed after her down into the interior of the bark.

2

UNDERSEA

SERAFIN AND EFT FOLLOWED THE MERMAIDS DOWN INTO the depths of the ocean.

Both wore diving helmets, transparent spheres that fastened around the neck with a leather band. But what looked like glass was actually hardened water, a legacy of the suboceanic kingdoms, which had collapsed thousands of years before. When Serafin hesitated to entrust his life to the sleek sphere, Eft explained to him that Merle had also swum through the canals of Venice using such a helmet; it was how she'd escaped the henchmen of the Empire.

Serafin had taken a few deep breaths before he put the helmet over his head, only to discover immediately that it wasn't necessary—he could breathe without difficulty under the hardened water, which nevertheless felt like glass. The sphere didn't even steam up on the inside. And after he'd survived the first moments of doubt and rising panic, he got used to it astonishingly quickly.

He and Eft had shaken hands with all the companions, even Lalapeya. The sphinx was continuing to maintain her human form. Then they'd climbed down to the mermaids in the water. Serafin's clothing became sodden with water right away, but not one drop came through the leather band at his neck. He was convinced that the helmets were magic; and if ancient techniques were in fact the reason behind them, they'd long been forgotten, along with their masters.

He'd pictured their descent into the sea witch's kingdom as a fantastic journey through the deep, breathtaking views over coral reefs, intertwining plants, and unknown creatures. Swarms of millions of fish, shimmering and colorful and of piercing beauty.

Instead they were greeted by darkness.

The light from the surface vanished after a few yards. First the surroundings turned dark green, then black. He could no longer see Eft, nor the two mermaids who drew them steeply downward by their hands. The pressure on his body hurt, but nothing more seemed to harm him, which contradicted practically all the theories he'd heard about diving to such depths. It was really naive to ascribe all this to the effect of the helmet, he knew that only too well, but what other choice did he have?

The wall of blackness around him was complete; he couldn't even see his own arms. He might as well have been able to float down bodiless. And perhaps it was exactly that: You gave your body to the coat check at the entrance to the kingdom of the sea witch the way you would elsewhere divest yourself of top hat and coat. It irritated him—no, in truth it frightened him terribly—that he and Eft could no longer see the mermaids, although he kept on feeling their hands. And what if that was only his imagination? What if he'd been floating down alone for a long time, into an abyss of cold and darkness and God knew what sort of creatures?

Don't think about it. Don't drive yourself crazy. Everything is all right. Everything will turn out well.

He called up the memory of Merle's face, her smile, the courage and flash in her eyes, the brave expression around her lips, and her untamable wild hair. He simply had to see her again. For that he would even put up with meeting a sea witch.

Under him—in front of him?—over him?—diffuse lights appeared in the blackness. As they came closer they looked like, yes, like *torches.*

Soon he realized that his guess was very close to the

truth. At wide intervals there were globes hanging in the sea, not firm ones, like his helmet, but wavering, constantly changing their form: air bubbles. And in the bubbles burned fire.

Fire in the deep sea, dozens, hundreds of fathoms under the surface!

By the gleam of the torches he could now make out his companions again, pale apparitions with long hair, women whose hips extended into lithe, scaly tails. Even behind the curtain of floating clouds of particles and inky strands of shadow, their faces would have been of flawless beauty—had it not been for their broad mouths, stretching from one ear to the other and studded with a quantity of razor-sharp teeth. Yet it wasn't the shark's jaws of the mermaids that drew his gaze again and again but their strikingly beautiful eyes.

The air bubbles with flames licking at their curves were now more frequent, and soon he saw the bottom of the sea. The ground was rocky, with extreme variations in height. The light bubbles bobbed gently up and down on bizarre fish bones and spikes, awakened to life by invisible currents, while the deep clefts and canyons lost themselves in blackness. Soon he could recognize that the surfaces of the undersea mountains themselves were covered with structures, ruins of walls, of buildings, of streets and alleys. Whether this place had at one time lain above the water or its inhabitants had lived here like fish remained uncertain. It was clear that this city had been abandoned a long time ago.

If it had been a part of the suboceanic kingdoms, that took away a little of its mystery, Serafin thought—whoever had lived here couldn't have been very much different from ordinary men, for their requirements were the same: walls to hide behind, streets in order not to lose their way, protection behind stone and metal.

The sea witch resided on a cliff, high over the sunken rock country.

She twined like a white worm in the darkness, fire bubbles dancing around her like fireflies—and yet, bafflingly, she escaped their glow, as if her skin were able to protect itself from reflecting the light.

She blew out an air bubble, as large as the freight hold of a trading frigate. She beckoned Serafin and Eft with thin, slender-boned hands. Her long hair floated around her head like a forest of water plants, waving and floating, without ever sinking back onto her shoulders.

She was as large as a mighty tower, even larger than her rival's corpse, which Serafin and the others had discovered on the surface. Her face united the beauty of the mermaids with the menace of a giant octopus.

The air bubble wafted toward Serafin and Eft. Just before it reached the two of them, the mermaids left their sides and whisked away with a few skillful flicks of their scaled tails. Serafin tried to avoid the bubble, but it touched him and drew him inside it. With a gasp he slid down its curve and came to lie at the bubble's deepest point. A moment later Eft landed beside him. She still wore the small knapsack with Arcimboldo's mirror mask on her back, from which nothing and no one could separate her. The straps were fastened so tightly that they cut into her shoulders.

The face of the witch appeared out of the darkness. She formed her lips into a kind of pucker, with which she sucked the bubble toward her. Her gigantic features came closer and closer, finally were as big as a house. Serafin tried to shrink back, but his hands and feet found no hold on the slippery bottom of the bubble. He could only sit there and wait as they steadily approached the witch's mouth.

"She's going to suck us in."

"No, I don't think so." Spellbound, Eft's eyes were fixed on the mighty face, terrible and beautiful at the same time.

"Sea witches are man-eaters," he said doggedly. "Every child knows that."

"Carrion-eaters, that's the difference. They eat dead men, not living ones."

"And who's to keep her from fixing that little flaw with a snap of her fingers?"

"If she wanted to kill us, she could have done it on the surface. But she's just vanquished another sea witch and taken over her kingdom. Maybe she's in a good mood—as far as you can say such a thing about a sea witch."

The face was now about ten yards away. A dozen fire

bubbles slid forward and flickered around the witch's head like a crown. Serafin stared only at her lips, full and dark, no broad slit like the mouth of the mermaids. Behind the lips, teeth gleamed brightly, long and sharp as fence posts.

The wall of the bubble bent in under the witch's features—nose, mouth, and eyes broke in and suddenly were directly in front of Serafin and Eft. The witch had pulled the bubble over her face like a mask. Water ran over her white-gray skin, broad rivulets flowing from the bridge of her nose down to the corners of her mouth and to her chin.

She had the face of a young woman, enlarged to absurdity as if under a magnifying glass. To look her in the eyes was to look so quickly from right to left that Serafin became dizzy, they were so far apart.

Eft had given up any attempt to stand. She remained sitting and did her best to indicate a bow. Serafin gathered that the same was expected of him, and so he did it.

The sea witch looked down at them, a wall of mouth and eyes and grisly teeth. "I welcome you to the under-sea." Her voice was not as loud as Serafin had feared, but the smell that came across her lips pressed him back against the bubble wall like a hot squall. Within seconds the inside of the bubble smelled like a slaughterhouse in the Calle Pinelli. The odor even came through the diving helmet. "What has brought you into my realm?"

"A flight," said Eft straight out.

"From whom?"

"You know what times we live in, Mistress. And from whom men flee."

The witch nodded only slightly, but the movement made the entire bubble tilt and threw Serafin and Eft together. One of the gigantic mouth corners rose in amusement. "The Egyptians, then. But you are no human."

"No. However, I live among them."

"You have the mouth of a mermaid. How can the humans ever accept you as one of their own?"

"I was young when I left the water. I did not know what I did."

"Who took your tail from you?"

"You must smell her scent on me."

Again the witch nodded, and again Serafin and Eft slithered around like insects that a child has trapped in a jar. "I killed her. She was old and stupid and full of evil thoughts."

Serafin thought of the corpse of the witch on the surface. He was amazed at the words of the creature before him. He couldn't have imagined that a sea witch could label something like that evil at all. Or would want to. *They are carrion-eaters,* Eft had said. But did that make them bad by nature? Men also ate dead meat.

"I was never a servant to your rival," Eft said to the witch. "It was a business deal. She was paid for exchanging my scaled tail for legs."

"I will believe that. When she died, she had no servants left. Even some of the other witches feared her."

"Then it was good that you conquered her."

The witch made an encircling movement deep under Serafin and Eft with her tree-size hands. "You know who once lived in this kingdom?"

Eft nodded. "The suboceaners were powerful in this area of the undersea."

"There is still an enormous amount to discover. The ruins of the suboceanic cultures are full of riddles. But I would have a greater compulsion to find them out if I did not have to worry about the Egyptians."

"Why should a being like you have to fear the Pharaoh?"

The witch allowed herself a real smile for the first time. "You need not flatter me, mermaid-with-legs. True, I am powerful here in the undersea. But that which gives the Egyptians power could also become dangerous to me sometime. And yet I do not fear for myself only. The Empire has almost exterminated the mermaids. We sea witches are born to rule, but over whom shall we rule if our subjects become ever fewer? Someday there will be no more mermaids, and then our hour has also come. The sea will become an empty, dead kingdom, full of fish with no understanding."

"Then hatred of the Egyptians unites us," said Eft.

"I do not hate them. I recognize their necessity in the course of things. But that does not mean that I will come to terms with them. With all the anger and the sorrow they have caused me." For a moment the gaze of the huge witch eyes was turned inward, lost in thought and heavy with care. Just as quickly her attention returned to the here and now. "What will you do if I let you go?"

Serafin had remained quiet for the entire time, and now, too, he thought the most reasonable thing was to leave the talking to Eft. She knew best how to deal with such a being. "The humans who are with me will die of thirst on the wide sea," said Eft. "And I do not want to go on alone. I would rather die."

"Great words," said the witch. "You mean them seriously, don't you?"

Eft nodded.

"What is your goal?"

Yes, thought Serafin, *what really is our goal?*

"Egypt," said Eft.

Serafin stared at her. The witch noticed it.

"Your companion is of another opinion?" The question was formulated as if it were addressed to Eft, but in fact the witch was now looking at Serafin, and she was expecting that he would give an answer.

"No," he said uncertainly. "By no means."

Eft gave him the shadow of a smile. Turning to the witch, she said, "Our only choices are hiding or fighting. I will fight. And I am sure my friends will choose the same course once they have the opportunity to think about it."

"You intend to attack Egypt?" asked the witch scornfully. "You alone?"

Serafin thought of the small troop waiting for them on

the surface of the water. He guessed that Dario, Aristide, and Tiziano would join them. But Lalapeya? She was a sphinx, even if she'd assumed the form of a human. Already, in Venice, she'd taken a stand against her people and so against the Empire, but the defeat had worn her out. He wasn't sure that she was ready to carry on the fight now. Or what sort of a reason she might have for it.

Anyway, what did that really mean, "fight"? What would that look like? The witch was right: At best they were six—against the combined power of the Pharaoh and the sphinx commanders.

Again the witch put the question to Eft: "You want to attack Egypt?"

Eft smiled, but the effect was grim. "We will find ways to injure them. Even if it's small things: a raid here, a dead priest there. A leaking ship, perhaps a dead sphinx once in a while."

"Nothing of that will even reach the ear of the Pharaoh," said the witch, "not to mention worry him."

"That doesn't matter. The act counts, not the result. You must understand that, Mistress. Did you not speak of exploring the ruins of the suboceanic kingdoms? What's your purpose in that? They will not rise again in their old glory. No result—only the will to do it. Just as with us."

"Are you speaking of obsession?"

"I would call it dedication."

The witch was silent, and the more minutes that passed,

the more convinced Serafin became that Eft had adopted the right tone. At the same time, it was clear to him that the mermaid had meant every word seriously. That frightened him a little, but he also admired her determination. She was right. He would go with her, no matter where.

"What is your name?" asked the witch finally.

Eft told her. Then she added, "And this is Serafin, the most skillful of the master thieves of Venice. And friend of the mermaids."

"You are mad, but you are also brave. That pleases me. You are a strong woman, Eft. A dangerous woman, for others and for yourself. Be careful that the scales don't tip too much to your side."

It had never occurred to Serafin that sea witches could be wise. Behind the fearsome facade there was far more than the bestial hunger for human flesh.

"Does that mean you are letting us go?" Eft spoke matter-of-factly, without any emotion.

"I am not only letting you go, I am going to help you."

The witch's words might have impressed Serafin, but that didn't mean he wanted her for a companion. No, not at all.

But the witch had something else in mind. "My handmaidens will take you back to your companions. Wait there for a while. Then you will find out what I mean."

And that was what happened.

The face of the witch withdrew from the bubble and sank into the darkness. Serafin discerned its warped outlines in the shadows one last time before the fire bubbles all around went out and the titanic being became one with the darkness.

They returned the way they had come. As they broke through the surface and saw the light of day over them, Serafin uttered a thankful sigh. Perhaps he wasn't the first human who'd survived an audience with a sea witch, but certainly one of the few. He'd learned as he listened to her, and his picture of the world had become yet a little more faceted, livelier, more varied. For that he was grateful to her.

Dario and the other boys helped them out of the water, up onto the floating corpse of the old sea witch. *Full of evil thoughts,* cried a voice from the deep into Serafin's mind, and now he found it even a little more disgusting to place his feet on the dead flesh of the corpse and to support himself on his hands while climbing up onto it.

Lalapeya awaited them on the ridge of the lifeless scaled tail. The sphinx did not smile, but she acted relieved. It was the first time since their flight from Venice that Serafin saw anything in her expression other than grief and sorrow.

They took turns reporting what had happened and were not interrupted by the others one single time. Even when Eft told what goal she'd named to the witch, no one argued.

Egypt, then, thought Serafin. And in an absurd, nightmarish way, it felt *right*.

An hour or two later the water began to boil, and something mighty rose from the sea.

3

The Heart of the Empire

The sunbark flew low, following the course of the frozen Nile. It was buffeted by the winter winds, but at least no snow was falling, which could have forced them down.

Merle gazed out through the window slits. Below them the land lay dazzlingly white. The once green banks of the Nile hardly contrasted with the desert anymore— everything was buried under a thick layer of snow. Here and there a frozen palm grove protruded from the ice, and sometimes she saw ruins of huts, the roofs crushed by the weight of the snow.

Where are all the people? she wondered.

"Frozen to death, perhaps," the Queen said in her thoughts.

Only perhaps? Merle asked.

"If the Pharaoh had not already incorporated them into his mummy armies."

You think he would have completely wiped out his own people to fill his army?

"You must not think of the Pharaoh as an Egyptian. He was a devil, even when he was alive more than four thousand years ago, but he has not been a human since the high priests awakened him. Whether the people who lived here on the Nile were ever his own is no longer of any consequence. Probably he saw no difference between the people here and those in all the other lands he conquered."

A land without people? But then who is he waging this war for?

"Not for the Egyptian people, that is certain. Perhaps not even for himself. You must not forget the influence of the priests of Horus on him."

Junipa was leaning on the wall of the bark beside Merle, her knees drawn up and her arms around them. Merle felt that Junipa was observing her, sometimes openly, sometimes covertly. Seth had fallen into a kind of trance after the bark's takeoff, which was probably necessary to steer the flight. Merle had observed him for a long while; then she'd decided to use the opportunity to tell Junipa everything that had happened since they'd parted at Arcimboldo's in Venice. The girl with the mirror eyes listened, passively at first, then with increasing interest. But she said nothing, asked no questions, and now Junipa was sitting there, and Merle could virtually feel what was going on in her friend's mind, as if Junipa were waiting for a sign of the Flowing Queen.

Merle's eyes wandered over to Seth, who sat on a pedestal in the front part of the bark, his face turned toward the inner space. A vein stood out on his forehead and disappeared beneath the golden network. Nevertheless, Merle thought she felt him groping toward her with invisible feelers. Once before, at their first encounter, she'd had the feeling that he was looking straight into her interior—and that he saw who was hidden there.

She wondered whether the Queen shared her perceptions, but this time she received no answer. The thought that even the Flowing Queen could be afraid of the most powerful of the Horus priests frightened her.

Seth was steering the bark by the power of his thoughts. The golden vehicle floated almost one hundred feet over the pack ice of the Nile, not very fast, for the cover of snow clouds over them was unbroken and no sunbeam pierced it. The diffuse daylight was enough to keep the bark in the air, but it wasn't strong enough to speed it up.

Merle had assumed that there would be strange equipment inside the bark and a sort of console like the ones in the steamboats that crossed the Venetian lagoons. But there was nothing like that. The interior was empty, the metal walls bare. They hadn't even installed benches—comfort was of no value to the undead mummy troops usually transported in the barks. The airship had all the charm of a prison cell.

Vermithrax stood right in front of Seth and kept his eyes on the priest. He'd folded his wings, but his claws were extended the entire time. His lava glow filled the interior of the bark with radiant brightness, which was reflected from the metal walls. The golden glow burned in Merle's eyes, even penetrating through the lids; she felt as if she'd been enclosed in amber.

Junipa had her eyes closed, but Merle knew that she could see anyway. With her mirror eyes she looked out through the lids, in the light as well as in darkness, and if Professor Burbridge had told the truth, she was also able to see into other worlds with them. That was more than Merle could imagine. More than she *wanted* to imagine.

The task of telling Seth the truth about the new ice age had fallen to Merle, of course. Vermithrax would rather have had his eyeteeth pulled than to fulfill a wish for the hated priest.

And so Merle had told the story of Winter, the mysterious albino whose life she'd saved in Hell. Winter, who'd insisted he was a season become flesh, searching for his missing love, Summer. She'd vanished years ago, he said, and since then there'd no longer been any real summer in the world, no July heat and no brooding sun in August. In Hell, Winter was only an ordinary human, but he'd told how on the surface he brought ice and snow with him, under which he buried the land. Winter could touch no living creature without freezing that being to ice in an instant. Only Summer, his beloved Summer, withstood this curse and nullified it with her singeing heat. Only those two could lie in each other's arms without killing one another, and it was their fate to belong to each other forever.

But now Summer was gone and Winter was searching for her.

Professor Burbridge—or Lord Light, as he was called as the ruler of Hell—must have given Winter a clue that lured him here to Egypt for the first time in thousands of years. In his wake, snowstorms had smoothed out the dunes and deadly ice lay over the desert.

There was no doubt that Winter had been here. Just like Merle, he'd left Hell through the steps inside the pyramid. But where did his path lead? Toward the north, apparently, for Seth was steering the bark northward, and as yet there was no end to the snow.

Seth had listened to her report and not interrupted her once. What was going on in his head remained his secret. But he'd kept his word: He'd gotten the bark into the air and so saved their lives. He'd even succeeded in producing a dry warmth inside the airship, which came from the gold layer on the walls.

"*He knows more about Winter than he is admitting,*" said the Queen.

Where do you get that? Merle asked in her thoughts. Her ability to speak soundlessly with the Queen had improved markedly in the days since their descent into Hell. She always found it easier to form the words with her lips, but she'd gotten quite good at the other way too, when she concentrated.

"*He is the second man of the Empire, the deputy of the Pharaoh,*" said the Queen. "*If the Egyptians have something to do with Summer's disappearance, he must know about it.*"

Summer is here?

"*Well, Winter is in Egypt. And he will have a good reason for it.*"

Merle looked over at Seth once again. With his closed eyes and relaxed facial expression he had lost something of his external menace. All the same, she did not for one second harbor the illusion that he could have anything else in mind except killing them all at the end of their journey. Their lives would depend on Vermithrax's getting to him first. The battle between the lion and the priest was unavoidable.

Seth's words had hit Vermithrax in a place that was vulnerable, despite all his strength. The words had sown doubt in him, doubt in that one bright spot that had given him hope of a better future. The reunion with his people, whom he'd long ago left behind somewhere in Africa, had always been the goal for Vermithrax, the end point of his journey. And now he was nagged by the fear that Seth might have spoken the truth, that the talking stone lion people had been extinguished by the Empire.

Merle turned to the Flowing Queen again: Do you think that's true?

"The Empire would be capable of it."

But the lions are so strong. . . .

"Other peoples were too. And they were more numerous than the free lions. Nevertheless, every single one of them was killed or enslaved."

Merle looked out the window. Who were they fighting for, actually, if there was no one left out there in the world? In an absurd way, that linked them to the Pharaoh: They were all engaged in a battle whose real goal they had long lost sight of.

Seth opened his eyes. "We'll be there soon."

"Where?" asked Merle.

"At the Iron Eye."

"What's that?" Merle had assumed that he was taking them to Heliopolis, the Pharaoh's capital city. Perhaps even to Cairo or Alexandria.

"The Iron Eye is the fortress of the sphinxes. From there they watch over Egypt." His tone was disparaging, and for the first time it occurred to Merle that Seth might be ruled by other motives than the absolute will for power. "The Iron Eye is in the Nile delta. It will come into sight soon."

Merle turned to her window slit again. If they were that far north, they must already have flown over Cairo. Why hadn't she seen anything of it? The snow was piled high, but not high enough to bury a city of millions of people.

It must be, then, that someone had leveled Cairo. Had there possibly been some resistance by the Egyptian people after the Pharaoh and the priests of Horus had seized power? The idea that Cairo and all its inhabitants had been annihilated took Merle's breath away.

Junipa's voice snatched her from her thoughts. "What do you want with the sphinxes?" she asked the priest.

Seth looked at Junipa for a long moment, expressionless. Then he smiled suddenly. "You are a clever child. No wonder they put the mirror eyes in you. Your friends were probably asking themselves what *they* were supposed to do in the Iron Eye. But you ask what drives *me* there. And that's just what it comes down to, isn't it?"

Merle wasn't sure she understood what he was talking about. She glanced at her friend, but Junipa did not betray what was in her mind by any emotion. Only when she spoke again did Merle understand where she was going—and that in fact she was right about it.

"You don't like the sphinxes," Junipa said. "I can see that."

For a fraction of a second Seth appeared surprised. Then he immediately had himself under control again. "Possibly."

"You are not here because the sphinxes are your friends. You are not going to ask the sphinxes for help, to kill us."

"Do you really believe I need help for that?"

"Yes," said Vermithrax; it was the first time he'd spoken in hours. "I certainly do believe that, utterly."

The two antagonists fixed each other in a stare, but neither went any further. Not here, not now.

Again it was Junipa who eased the tension. Her gentle, infinitely relaxed voice groped for Seth's attention. "You tried to kill Lord Light, and you returned from Hell into a land that has turned into a desert of ice. Why didn't you make your way to the court of the Pharaoh first or to the temple of the Horus priests? Why straight to the stronghold of the sphinxes? That is quite remarkable, I think."

"And what, in your opinion, might all that mean, little mirror maiden?"

"A fire in your heart," she said enigmatically.

Merle stared at Junipa before her eyes met those of the obsidian lion. For a moment, amazement drove the coldness out of Vermithrax's eyes.

Seth tilted his head. "Fire?"

"Love. Or hate." Junipa's mirror eyes glowed in the golden shine of the lion. "More likely hate."

The priest was silent, thinking.

Junipa spoke again: "Vengeance, I think. You hate the sphinxes, and you are here to destroy them."

"*By all the gods!*" murmured the Flowing Queen in Merle's mind.

Vermithrax was still listening intently, and his eyes moved from Junipa back to Seth. "Is that true?"

The priest of Horus paid no attention to the lion. Not even Merle, whom he'd observed constantly before, appeared to have any importance for him now. It was as if he were alone in the bark with Junipa.

"You are actually an astonishing creature, little girl."

"My name is Junipa."

"Junipa," he repeated slowly. "Quite astonishing."

"You're no longer the right hand of the Pharaoh, are you? You lost everything when you didn't succeed in killing Lord Light down there." Junipa thoughtfully turned a strand of her white-blond hair between thumb and forefinger. "I know that I'm right. Sometimes I see not only the surface but also the heart of the matter."

Seth sighed deeply. "The Pharaoh betrayed the Horus priests. He gave me the commission to murder Lord Light. The sphinxes prophesied to Amenophis that someone would come out of Hell and kill him. Therefore he intended that I should kill Lord Light—and best that I should also die while doing it. Amenophis had all my priests taken prisoner and threatened to kill them if my mission was not successful."

"Now," said Vermithrax with pleasure, "you are ruined. My congratulations."

Seth glared at him, but he made no reply. Instead he continued, "I am certain that Amenophis already knows that Lord Light is still alive." He lowered his eyes, and Merle almost wished she could feel pity for him. "My priests are now dead. The cult of Horus exists no more. I am the only one left. And the sphinxes have taken our place at the side of the Pharaoh. It was planned thus from the beginning: We should awaken Amenophis again and lay the foundations of the Empire. The sphinxes are the ones who are now harvesting the fruits of all our labors. They waited in the background until the time was ripe to draw the Pharaoh to their side. They got him to betray us. The sphinxes used Amenophis, and they used *us*. We were manipulated without knowing it. Or, no, that's not right. Others warned me, but I threw their advice to the winds. I didn't want to believe that the sphinxes were playing a false game with the Empire. But it was always going toward one thing: The Empire conquers the world, and the sphinxes take over the Empire. They made us into their tools, and I was the most gullible of all, because I closed my eyes to the truth. My priests had to pay the price for my mistake."

"And now you are on the way to the sphinxes to avenge them," said Junipa.

Seth nodded. "*That,* at least, I can do."

"*My heart is quite heavy,*" the Queen remarked sarcastically.

Merle paid no attention to her. "How do you intend to annihilate the sphinxes?"

Seth appeared a little shocked at his own openness. He, the most powerful of the Horus priests, destroyer of countless lands and slaughterer of entire peoples, had openly spoken his thoughts to two children and an embittered stone lion.

"I don't know yet," he said after a moment of thoughtful silence. "But I will find a way."

Vermithrax snorted scornfully, but not as loudly as he would probably have done *before* Seth's avowal. The priest's candor had surprised him, too, even impressed him a little.

Nevertheless, no one made the mistake of considering Seth an ally. If it meant an advantage for him, he would sacrifice all of them at the first opportunity. This man had extinguished tens of thousands with a wave of his hand, had burned cities to the ground with a brief command, and desecrated the cemeteries of entire nations in order to make the bodies into mummy soldiers.

Seth was no ally.

He was the devil himself.

"*Good,*" said the Flowing Queen. "*And I was beginning to think he was going to wind all of you around his finger with his entertaining little tragedy.*"

Merle grasped Junipa's hand. "What more do you know about him?" she asked, disregarding Seth's blazing look.

The mirror eyes reflected Vermithrax's golden glow with such intensity that Merle's image in them glowed like an insect in a candle flame. "Seth is a bad man," said Junipa, "but the sphinxes are infinitely worse."

Seth gave a slight, scornful bow.

"That will look good on your tombstone," said Vermithrax grimly.

"I will order that it be chiseled out of your flank," returned the priest.

Vermithrax scraped one of his paws across the floor but refused to be drawn into another battle of words. He preferred a battle with sharp claws to such subtleties.

Merle regarded Junipa with growing concern for a long moment, but then her eyes strayed to the window—and beyond it the monstrosity that rose over the delta of ice.

"Is *that* the Iron Eye?"

Seth didn't look out, keeping his expressionless gaze on Merle. No one needed his confirmation. They all knew the answer.

Junipa also pressed her face against the narrow glass. Ice patterns had formed around the edges of the windows, finely branching fingers that reached toward her mirror eyes.

It looked like a mountain, a pointed cone of ice and snow, an unnatural pucker in the flat landscape, as if someone had bunched the horizon together like a piece of paper. As they came closer, Merle could make out details. The image in front of them was pyramid-shaped, but with steep slopes, cut off at the top as if someone had struck off the point with a scythe, and there, in place of the point, peeling itself out of the snowdrifts, was a collection of towers and gables, balconies, balustrades, and arcades of columns. Whatever was hidden in the interior of the Iron Eye, that up there was the *true* eye. It seemed to Merle like the crow's nest of a gigantic ship, which could look out over the country and perhaps the entire Empire. The colossus—was it of steel or stone, or really made of iron?—appeared to Merle functional, without decoration, without any useless flourishes. But the upper buildings with which the fortress culminated sparkled in fantastic elegance: playful buildings with much decoration, narrow bridges, and extravagantly framed windows. If there was a place where the sphinxes really *lived*—not reigned, not commanded—then it was there at the tip of the Iron Eye.

The fortress was high, perhaps higher than the sky; but no, it was just that the cloud cover was hanging so gray and heavy over it, as it had everywhere on their journey. All-powerful the Iron Eye might be, but not supernatural, not heavenly.

He is a bad man, but the sphinxes are infinitely worse.

Merle heard Junipa's words about Seth once more, a whispering echo in her thoughts.

The bark circled in a wide arc around the whole area. Merle was not sure what Seth was intending by that. Did he mean to impress them with a final glorification of his magic powers? Or did he want them to see the power of the sphinxes along with the fortress? A warning?

Finally he guided the bark toward one of the countless openings in the south side of the eye, horizontal slits in the snow-covered white of the steep side. As they approached, Merle could see a whole squadron of sunbarks inside.

A dozen reconnaissance craft circled around the fortress, keeping the frozen arms of the river delta under surveillance. Yet their movements were sluggish, the cloudy sky having robbed the dreaded sunbarks of their agility. The birds of prey had turned into lame ducks.

"What are you going to do now?" Merle asked.

Seth closed his eyes again, concentrating on the landing. "I must land the bark in the hangar."

"But they'll see us when we disembark."

"That's not my problem."

Vermithrax took a step toward Seth. "It could easily become yours."

Once more the priest opened his eyes, but his gaze was directed toward Junipa, not at the lion who threatened him. "I could try to land up on the platform. The patrols will see it, but if we have any luck, we would already have disappeared between the buildings by that time."

"*Why is he risking his life for us?*" the Queen asked mistrustfully.

"That's a trick," growled Vermithrax also.

Seth shrugged, now with his eyes closed again. "Do you have a better suggestion?"

"Take us away from here, now," said the lion.

"And the truth you are seeking?" Seth smiled. "Where else will you find it?"

Vermithrax was silent then. Merle and Junipa said nothing more either. They had the choice between being set down in the snow again or hiding somewhere in the Iron Eye until they'd agreed on a reasonable plan.

Just before the hangar opening, the bark swerved, rose, and floated upward in a broad spiral. Merle tried to keep the patrols in sight, but her vision was limited by the narrow window slits, and she could make out only a single flying sickle in the distance. Finally she gave up. She had to resign herself to the fact that at the moment her life lay in Seth's hands alone.

The bark needed several minutes to reach its target. Merle turned to the other side of the airship so that she could look at the buildings more closely. Thick caps of snow lay on all the roofs, balconies, and projections, and the vacant edge of the platform was so deeply snowed in that Merle questioned whether they could leave the bark at all there. It would be next to impossible to run away from their opponents in the deep snow.

Seth let the sunbark sink to the ground. It landed gently on the snow, accompanied by the crunching and snapping of the icy crust. The first buildings were more than twenty yards away from them. Through the window slits Merle saw narrow, deep lanes between the buildings. Considering the numerous roofs and towers, there must be a real labyrinth of lanes and streets in there.

Involuntarily Merle thought of Serafin. Of how, as a master thief, he would have known how best to move inconspicuously through such a maze of streets.

Of how very much she missed him.

"Get out of here!" Seth's voice wiped Serafin's face from her thoughts. "Quick, *get moving!*"

And then she ran. With Junipa by the hand. Occasionally without her too. Then with her again. Stumbling. Freezing. Without daring to look up, for fear she might see a bark diving down at her.

Only when they'd taken cover behind a wall, one after the other and even Seth and Vermithrax almost harmoniously side by side, did Merle dare breathe again.

"What now?" The lion was staring tensely at the edge of the platform, where the glittering snow field ended abruptly in front of the gray of the cloud background.

"You can go where you want to." Seth cast a sideways look first at Merle, then at Junipa. It didn't escape Merle how piercingly he kept examining Junipa, before in the bark and now here outside, and she didn't like it at all.

Junipa herself didn't notice. She had placed a hand flat on the wall of the building, and now a suppressed groan came from her throat. With a jerk she pulled her arm back and stared at her palm—it was red as fire, and on the palm glowed droplets of blood.

"Iron," said Vermithrax, while Merle bent over Junipa's hand worriedly. "The walls are actually made of iron."

Seth smiled to himself.

The lion sniffed a finger's breadth away from the wall. "Don't touch! The cold will make your skin stick to it." And then he seemed to remember that Junipa had already made exactly that mistake. "Everything all right?" he asked in her direction.

Merle had used her sleeve to blot the blood from Junipa's hand. It wasn't much, and it didn't keep flowing. Junipa was lucky. Except in a few places where the thin outer layer of skin had peeled off and was still stuck to the iron, she wasn't injured. In a normal person it would have taken one or two days until she could clench her fist again, but Junipa carried the Stone Light in her. Merle had seen with her own eyes how quickly Junipa's wounds healed.

"It'll be all right," she said softly.

Seth shoved Merle aside, took Junipa's hand in his, whispered something, and then let it go again. Afterward the redness paled, and the edges of the shredded skin had closed.

Merle stared at the hand. Why did he do that, she thought. Why is he helping us?

"Not us," said the Flowing Queen. *"Junipa."*

What does he want from her?

"I do not know."

Merle wasn't sure she wanted to believe her. The Queen still had too many secrets from her, and if she thought about it carefully, new riddles were constantly appearing. Merle didn't even take the trouble to hide these thoughts from her invisible guest. The Queen might as well know that she didn't trust her.

"Seth is playing a double game," said the Queen. Again mistrust rose in Merle. Was the Queen trying to divert attention from herself?

The priest had turned away from the little group and hastened, stooping, through the snow to a door that led into the interior of the building: a high tower with a flat roof, whose upper surface was covered with a bizarre pattern of ice tracery. At first look, it wasn't possible to see that under the crust of frost was concealed polished metal.

"Wait!" Vermithrax called after the Horus priest, but Seth acted as if he hadn't heard the lion. Just before the door he stopped and looked behind him briefly.

"I don't need the extra baggage of children and *animals.*" The way he emphasized the word was an open challenge. "Do what you want, but don't run after me."

Merle and Junipa exchanged a look. It was too cold out

here, the wind was as cutting as broken glass. They had to get inside the fortress, no matter what Seth thought about it.

With two sliding steps Vermithrax was beside the priest and shoved him aside, a bit more roughly than necessary. When he noticed that the door was barred, he pushed it in with a blow of his paw. Merle realized that the lock had broken and the door was made of wood. Only the outer surface was overlaid with a reflective metal alloy. Perhaps the walls were made the same way and were not really of massive iron, as she'd supposed until now. She wasn't at all sure if ordinary iron could reflect like that; probably it was some other metal. Real iron existed only in the name of the fortress.

"That was certainly discreet," Seth observed mockingly as he walked past Vermithrax into the interior of the building. Beyond lay a short corridor, which led into a stairwell.

Everything was silvery and reflective, the walls, the floor, the ceiling. Inside, the mirrors were no longer of metal but of glass. They saw themselves reflected in the walls of the passages, clear as glass, without any noticeable distortions. Since the mirror walls on both sides of the corridors lay opposite each other, their likeness continued into infinity, a whole army of Merles, Junipas, Seths, and obsidian lions.

Vermithrax's glow shone in the multiplication as brightly as a sun, a whole chain of suns, and what had been quite useful to them up till now—a constant source of light, entirely without lamps or torches—became a treacherous alarm signal to anyone who approached them.

The stairs were wider than in a human building. The intervals had to fit the four lion paws of a sphinx, and the height of the individual steps was also enormous. For Vermithrax, however, the unusual dimensions were an advantage, and so he took Merle and Junipa on his back and observed with satisfaction how Seth was soon sweating with exertion.

"Where are we going, actually?" Merle asked.

"*I would like to know that too,*" said the Queen.

"Down," retorted Seth, who was walking in front.

"Oh?"

"I didn't ask you to come with me."

Vermithrax tapped him on the shoulder with the tip of his wing. "Where?" he asked with emphasis.

The priest stopped, and for a few instants such fury blazed in his eyes that Merle felt Vermithrax's muscles tense under his coat. She wasn't even sure if it actually was only fury that raged in the priest's head: Perhaps it was magic—black, evil, lethal magic.

But Seth laid no spell on them. Instead he glared at Vermithrax for a moment longer, then said softly, "Soon it will be swarming with sphinxes up here. Someone will notice that we landed on the platform. And I don't want to be here when that happens. Farther down it's easier to hide. Or do you think in all seriousness that sphinxes are dumb enough to overlook thousands of lions who shine like the full moon and perhaps have as much intelligence?" And with that he pointed to the endless line of Vermithrax's reflections all around them in the stairwell.

Before the obsidian lion could reply, Seth was on his way again. Vermithrax snorted and followed him. As they rocked quickly downward, Merle observed herself and Junipa in the mirrors. It gave her a headache and made her dizzy, and yet she could not escape the fascination of this apparent endlessness.

She remembered again the magic water mirror in her pocket and the mirror ghost who'd been trapped inside since the beginning of her journey. She pulled the shimmering oval out and looked at it. Junipa was looking over her shoulder.

"You still have it," Junipa stated.

"Sure."

"Do you remember how I looked into it?"

Merle nodded.

"And I wouldn't tell you what I saw in the mirror?"

"Are you going to tell me now?" asked Merle.

They both looked for a moment longer at the wavering surface of the water mirror, at their own wobbling faces.

"A sphinx," Junipa said softly, so that Seth could not hear her. "There was a sphinx on the other side. A woman with the body of a lion."

Merle let the mirror sink, until its cool back touched her thigh. "Seriously?"

"I don't make jokes," said Junipa sadly. "Not anymore, not for a long time."

"But why—" Merle broke off. Until now she'd believed that the hand that reached for hers on the other side of the water mirror when she shoved her fingers into it belonged to her mother. The mother she had never known.

But—a sphinx?

"Perhaps it was something like a warning?" she said. "A sort of look into the future?"

"Perhaps." Junipa didn't sound convinced. "The sphinx was standing in a room full of billowing yellow curtains. She was very beautiful. And she had dark hair, just like you."

"What are you trying to say?"

Junipa hesitated. "Nothing . . . I think."

"Yes, you are."

"I don't know."

"Do you really think my mother was a sphinx?" She swallowed and tried to laugh at the same time, but it failed miserably. "That's just nonsense."

"What I saw *was* a sphinx, Merle. I didn't say it was your mother. Or anyone else you had to know."

Merle regarded the mirror in silence; it had accompanied her all her life and she had always guarded it like the apple of her eye. Her parents had laid it in the wicker basket in which she'd been set out on Venice's canals as a newborn. It had always been the only link to her origins, the only clue. But now it seemed to her that its reflection was a little darker, a little stranger.

"I shouldn't have said anything," said Junipa, downcast.

"Yes, you were right to."

"I didn't want to frighten you."

"I'm glad I know." But what did she know, really?

Junipa shook her head behind Merle's shoulder. "Perhaps it was only some old image. Neither of us has any idea what it means."

Merle sighed, but as she was about to put the mirror away, she again remembered the ghost trapped inside, a milky film that rushed back and forth over the watery surface. "Do you think it could be that phantom from Arcimboldo's mirrors?"

Gently she touched the surface with her fingertip. Not deep enough to poke through the surface. Very, very gently.

"There is someone here," said the Flowing Queen.

Silence.

"Everywhere," said the Flowing Queen, and for a moment she sounded almost panicked. *"He . . . he is here!"*

"Here?" Merle whispered.

Vermithrax noticed that something was happening on his back and briefly lowered his head, without, however, looking back so as not to make Seth aware of the two girls' activity.

"Hello?" Merle whispered.

A syllable sounded in her mind, then the sound blurred, whispering and hissing.

Was that you? she asked the Queen, although she already guessed the answer.

"No."

She tried again, with the same experience. The voice from the mirror was too unclear. Merle knew why: Her fingers had poked too deeply into the water of the mirror. It was impossible while they were going down the stairs to stay still enough—but that's exactly what seemed to be needed to hear the voice of the ghost. She was angry with herself for not having tried it sooner. But when? Since her flight from Venice she hadn't ever had a single quiet moment, no real breather.

"Later," she whispered, drew out her finger, and let the mirror disappear into the buttoned pocket once more. To Junipa she said, "It won't work here. It's too wobbly."

"Something's not right," Seth said at the same time.

Vermithrax slowed. "What do you mean?"

"Why aren't we meeting anyone?"

"It's said that the sphinx population isn't very large," said Merle with a shrug. "At least, someone told us that."

"That is true," said Seth. "No more than two or three hundred. They don't reproduce anymore."

"They never have," said the Queen.

How do you know so much about them? Merle asked.

"Old reports." For the first time Merle felt very clearly that the Queen was lying.

Seth went on, "But there are still enough left to populate their own stronghold."

"If the barks are being piloted by sphinxes these days, a whole lot of them must be gone," Merle said.

"But even if you take away the ones who are in Venice or at the court in Heliopolis, there must still be far more than a hundred in the fortress. It's unusual for everything to be so dead."

"Maybe we should be glad about it instead of pulling a long face," suggested Vermithrax, who by nature had to oppose everything that came from Seth.

The priest lowered his voice. "Yes, perhaps."

"Anyhow, there were patrols outside," said Merle. "So the sphinxes must be in here somewhere."

Seth nodded and went on. They might now have gone some one hundred and fifty feet downward, but still there was no end to the stairs. A few times Merle managed to look over the railing, but only more and more mirrors shimmered up at her from below. It was impossible to see the bottom of the staircase.

And then, unexpectedly, they got to the end.

The stairwell opened into a large room, mirrored like all the others in this fortress. The walls consisted of countless mirror surfaces like the faceted eye of an insect.

"I wonder who polishes them all," Merle murmured,

but she was only covering up the fear that the surroundings aroused in her. The room might be approximately round and empty, but the mirrors reflecting each other a thousand times made it impossible to determine its dimensions clearly. They might just as well be going through a mirror labyrinth of narrow corridors. Vermithrax's glow, beaming back at them from all directions, didn't make things any easier, and it constantly blinded them. Only Junipa was not disturbed by it; with mirror eyes of her own, she looked through the brightness and the illusion of the multiplications.

Someone yelled something.

For a moment Merle thought Seth had cried out. But then she realized the truth: They were surrounded.

What at first look appeared to be hundreds of sphinxes who approached them from all sides was soon revealed to be only one.

The dark-haired man with the lower body of a sand-yellow lion was broader in the shoulders than any of the harbor workers on the Venetian quays. He wore a sword lance as long as a man, its blade reflecting Vermithrax's golden glow. It looked like a torch.

Seth stepped forward and said something in Egyptian. Then he added so that all could understand, "Do you speak the language of my . . . friends?"

The sphinx nodded and weighed the sword lance in his hands for a moment, without lowering the point. His eyes kept darting uncertainly toward Vermithrax.

"You are Seth?" he asked the Horus priest in Merle's language.

"It is so. And I have the right to be here. Only the word of the Pharaoh weighs more heavily than mine."

The sphinx snorted. "The word of the Pharaoh commands that you be taken prisoner as soon as anyone sees you. Everyone knows that you have betrayed the Empire and are fighting on the side"—he hesitated—"of our enemies." His short pause was probably due to the fact that he couldn't imagine what enemies of the Empire were left after decades of war.

Seth bowed his head, which might have seemed submissive to the sphinx but in truth was preparation for—yes, what? A magic blow that would shred his opponent?

Merle was never to find out, for at that moment the sphinx received reinforcements. Behind him, through an almost invisible opening between the mirrors, a troop of mummy soldiers appeared. Their images multiplied in the walls like a chain of cut paper dolls being drawn apart by invisible hands.

The mummies wore armor of leather and steel, but even that could not conceal that these undead soldiers were specimens with uncommonly robust proportions. Their faces were ash gray, with dark rings under the eyes, but they did not appear as wasted and half decayed as other mummies of the Empire. Perhaps they hadn't been dead so long when they were snatched from their graves to serve in the Pharaoh's armies.

The soldiers moved into place behind the sphinx. Their mirror images made it hard to say how many there really were. Merle counted four, but perhaps she was wrong and there were more.

The air over the golden network that covered the back of Seth's head shimmered the way it does on an especially hot summer day.

Horus magic shot through Merle's mind, and at the same time she had to think that his magic could just as well be directed at them and not against their enemies.

At the same moment the mummy soldier in front raised his sickle sword. The sphinx looked back over his shoulder, visibly irritated by the appearance of the soldiers but at the same time grateful for their support. Then he turned again to Seth, Vermithrax, and the girls on the back of the lion. He now grasped that the Horus priest had not bowed to honor him, saw the boiling air over Seth's skull, raised his lance, about to launch it at the priest—

—and was felled from behind by the mummy soldier's sword blow.

Instantly the soldiers leaped over the sphinx lying on the ground and struck at him from all sides. When there was no more life in him, their leader turned slowly around. His eyes passed over Vermithrax and the girls, then fastened on Seth.

The network on the priest's skull glowed, and fireballs like balls of pure lava appeared in Seth's hands.

"No," said the mummy soldier. His voice sounded astonishingly alive. "We don't belong to them."

Seth hesitated.

"Let them alone, Seth," cried Merle. She didn't suppose the priest would pay any attention to her, but for some reason he still didn't throw the fireballs.

"They are not real," said the Queen in Merle's head.

The mummies?

"Not those, either. But I meant the fireballs. They are only illusion. The Horus priests understand that better than anyone: about lies, about deceit. And, in addition, about alchemy and the awakening of the dead."

Then he can't burn up the soldiers at all?

"Not with this playacting."

Merle let out a deep sigh. She watched the foremost mummy soldier raise his left hand and rub his face with it. The gray disappeared, the dark eye rings smeared.

"We are no more dead than you are," he said. "And before we all slaughter each other, we should at least find out if it would not be more reasonable to work together." The man spoke with a strong accent, his *r*'s sounding strangely hard and rolling.

Seth's fireballs went out. The air over his skull quieted.

"I think I know who they are," said the Queen. *"Merle, do you still remember what you found in the*

abandoned tent in the abyss of Hell? Before the Lilim appeared and destroyed everything?"

Merle needed a second or two before she realized what the Queen was getting at. The chicken's claw?

"Yes. Do you still have it?"

In my knapsack.

"Tell Junipa to get it out."

A moment later Junipa was fumbling with the fastenings of the knapsack.

"Who are you?" Vermithrax asked, and he took a threatening step forward. Seth stepped aside, becoming cautious and perhaps realizing that his illusions were inferior to the fangs and teeth of the lion.

"Spies," said the false mummy soldier.

Junipa fished the chicken's claw on its little leather band from Merle's knapsack and handed it forward to her.

The mummy soldier spotted it at once, as if Merle had waved a glowing torch at him.

"Spies from the kingdom of the Czar," he said, smiling.

4

PIRATES

SERAFIN WAS STANDING IN FRONT OF A ROUND PORTHOLE and watching the wonders of the sea bottom move past them. Swarms of fish sparkled in the semidarkness. He could make out undersea forests of bizarre growths and things that might perhaps be plants, perhaps animals.

The submarine that had taken them aboard on the sea witch's orders was gliding, raylike, through the deep, accompanied by dozens of fire bubbles such as they'd already seen at the witch's side. The glowing spheres were drawn along to the right and left of the boat like a swarm of comets, covering the sea bottom with a flaring pattern of light and dark.

Dario walked over to him. "Isn't this incredible?"

Serafin acted as if he'd been snatched from a deep dream. "This boat? Yes . . . yes, it really is."

"You don't sound especially enthusiastic."

"Have you seen the crew? And that madman who calls himself the captain?"

Dario gave him an amused smile. "You haven't figured it out yet, have you?"

"What?"

"They're pirates."

"Pirates?" Serafin uttered a soft groan. "How do you get that?"

"One of them told me while you were moping around here for hours at a time."

"I was thinking about Merle," Serafin said quietly. Then he frowned. "*Real* pirates?"

Dario nodded, and his grin became wider. Serafin wondered what made his friend so enthusiastic about the fact that they'd fallen into the hands of a band of robbers and murderers. Romantic dreams of piracy, perhaps; the old stories of noble freebooters who crossed the oceans of the world proudly and with no respect for authority.

The news didn't surprise Serafin especially. Dario's discovery fit right into the picture. What sort of an ally might they expect from a sea witch? Besides, Captain Calvino commanded his crew with a harshness that bordered on cruelty. And the sailors themselves? Recognizable as cutthroats, even from a distance, dark fellows with wild hair, dirty clothing, and innumerable scars.

Just terrific. Fantastic. Out of the frying pan, into the fire.

"They pay for the witch's protection with corpses," Dario said with relish.

"And I thought we'd all seen enough corpses," Serafin blazed at him.

Dario flinched. The memory of their flight from Venice and Boro's death was still fresh in his mind, and the comment obviously pained him. Serafin regretted his sharp retort: Dario's enthusiasm for the pirates was nothing but a masquerade behind which he hid his true feelings. Indeed, underneath it, he was suffering like all the others over what had happened.

Serafin laid a hand on his shoulder. "Sorry."

Dario managed a troubled smile. "My mistake."

"Tell me what else you found out." In a burst of harsh self-criticism, he added, "At least you were smart enough to find out more about our new 'friends,' instead of just staring stupidly out the window."

Dario nodded briefly, but then his grin was replaced by an uneasy look. He stepped up next to Serafin at the porthole, and both turned their faces to the glass.

"They collect the bodies of their victims in a space in the back part of the boat. But to be honest, I'm not sure there are any ships left up on the surface that could be robbed by pirates. They certainly wouldn't dare attack the Egyptian war galleys, and as far as I know, there hasn't been any trade to speak of in the Mediterranean since the beginning of the war."

Serafin nodded. The Empire had cut all the trade routes. In the deserted harbors there were no more customers for merchants. Like all the others, the traders, together with the crews of their ships, had landed in the mummy factories as slaves.

Dario cast a guarded look back into the room: They were in one of the narrow cabins, along whose bronze-colored walls ran a maze of pipes, artfully worked into extravagant decorations, similar to the plasterwork in Venetian palaces, with the single difference that the patterns here were made of metal and wood. Not for the first time, Serafin wondered whom Captain Calvino had seized the boat from. He most certainly had not designed it himself, for he did not appear to be the kind of man who appreciated beauty. And along with all the functionality of the undersea boat, it was obvious that someone with taste and an understanding of art had been at work here.

Besides the two boys, there were also two sailors in the cabin. One of them was pretending to be asleep in his berth, but Serafin had seen him blink and look in his direction several times. The second man let his legs dangle over the side of his bunk as he whittled the figure of a mermaid from a piece of wood; wood shavings fell into the empty berth below him. There were eight empty beds, and the boys knew that there were several of these crew quarters aboard the boat. Captain Calvino had quartered Serafin and Dario in this cabin, Tiziano and Aristide in another. Eft and Lalapeya were lodged in a double cabin at the end of the central passageway, which ran like a spinal column through the entire boat; it wasn't far from the captain's cabin.

At this hour most of the crew members were carrying out their duties in the labyrinthine spaces of the submarine. It was obvious that the two men in the berths had been placed there to keep an eye on the passengers, even if they took pains to appear uninterested. No one kept the boys from wandering around the boat, and yet they didn't take a step that was not observed. Captain Calvino might be an unscrupulous slave driver, but he was no fool. And not even the sea witch's unequivocal order to transport his guests to Egypt unharmed kept him from openly conveying his displeasure with that order.

In a whisper, Dario relayed what he'd learned: "The sea witch has placed the boat under her protection for as long as Calvino provides her with the flesh of corpses. They collect victims of shipwrecks and drownings all over the Mediterranean and bring them to the sea witch. The fellow I spoke with told me they dive around under the battlefields of the great sea wars all year long and catch the dead in nets. Appetizing job, eh? Oh, well, anyway, that's what they do, because piracy isn't going so well anymore.

No one, not even this madman Calvino, wants to get mixed up with the Egyptians. And if he isn't fishing bodies out of the water, he carries out commissions for the witch. Like getting us to Egypt."

"Do you know how they got this boat?"

"They said Calvino won it, together with the crew, in a dice game. No idea if that's true at all. If it is, you could probably figure he cheated, that so-and-so. Have you seen how he stares at Lalapeya?"

Serafin smiled. "To be honest, I'm not the least bit worried about her." The idea that Calvino might have the sphinx brought into his cabin was simply irresistible: Picturing the captain's dumb face when the sphinx took her true form and showed him her lion's claws was worth gold.

"Have you spoken with Tiziano and Aristide?" asked Serafin.

"Of course. They're wandering around in the boat somewhere and sticking their noses into everything that's none of their business."

Serafin's guilt deepened. The others had immediately started to become familiar with their new surroundings. Only he was spending valuable time indulging in his melancholy thoughts. The uncertainty over what had become of Merle troubled him more strongly the longer they were under way. But he mustn't let himself lose sight of the most important thing: to bring them all out of this story safe and sound.

"Serafin?"

"Umm." He blinked as Dario's face came into focus in front of him again.

"You aren't responsible for anyone here. Just don't talk yourself into that."

"I'm not."

"I think you are. You led us when we went into the Doge's palace. But that's long past. Out here, we're all in the same"—he grinned crookedly—"in the same boat."

Serafin sighed, then managed a weak smile. "Let's go up to the bridge. I'd rather look Calvino in the eye than sit around here not knowing if he's just given the order to cut all our throats." As they went to the door together, he called to the two men in the berths, "We're just going out for a few minutes to sabotage the machinery."

The sailor with the whittling knife stared in surprise at his comrade, who acted as if he were just awakening from a deep sleep with an unconvincing yawn.

Serafin and Dario made their way quickly down the passageway. Everywhere the sights they saw were similar: pipes and steam ducts, artfully integrated into the richly decorated walls and ceilings and thick with verdigris; oriental carpets torn by heavy boots; the curtains in front of some portholes gnawed by mildew and dampness; and chandeliers missing single crystals and even arms, fallen off at some time and never replaced. The former glory of the boat was long gone to ruin. Wooden moldings were gouged and spoiled with childish whittlings, some actually broken by fighting fists. Here and there glass doors were missing from cupboards and partitions. The ceilings and floor coverings were full of wine and rum spots. On some of the murals, the pirates had blackened teeth and added mustaches.

The bridge was in the top of the submarine, behind a double-sectioned window that looked out into the ocean deep like a pair of eyes. Captain Calvino, clothed in a rust red morning coat with a golden collar, was walking back and forth in front of the windshield, his hands clasped behind his back, arguing excitedly with someone who was blocked from Dario and Serafin's view by a column. Half a dozen men were working at wheels and levers, which, like most everything aboard, were made of brass; one man sat on an upholstered saddle and was pedaling furiously on a couple of pedals, which drove heaven knew what kind of a machine.

The two boys walked slowly up to the small platform in the front part of the bridge. Calvino did not interrupt his furious pacing for one second. As they approached, they discovered who was with him and quite obviously needling him to a white heat.

Eft saw the two boys at the same time. Her wide mermaid mouth was not covered by its usual mask. The knapsack in which she preserved Arcimboldo's mirror mask hung over her shoulder, as always, for Eft never let her precious possession out of her sight for a moment.

"I know boats like this," she said, now turning to Calvino again. "And I know how fast they can be. Faster anyway than what you're trying to fool us with here."

"I've already told you a thousand times, and I'll tell you once more," thundered the captain. The scar that split his lower lip and reached down to his Adam's apple showed white against his flushed face. "The Egyptians control the sea, and for a long time they haven't been content to just search for prey on the surface. To go faster, we have to go up, and I will not take that risk. The sea witch's commission says to take you and these children to Egypt—mad enough, by Neptune!—but she said nothing about the matter of being in such a hurry. So you will kindly leave it to me to decide what speed we travel at."

"You are a stubborn old goat, Captain, and I'm not the least surprised that you've let this marvel of a boat run down this way. We should probably consider ourselves lucky if we get to Egypt at all before your garbage heap of a tub breaks apart."

Calvino whirled around, came close to Eft, and stopped about six inches away from her. He stretched his scarred face toward her threateningly. Serafin was sure that Eft was now able to smell the remnants of meals in his dark beard. "You may be a woman or a fishwife or the devil knows what, but you will not tell me how to run my boat!"

Eft remained unimpressed, although she must also have seen the saber that dangled from the captain's belt.

Calvino had wrapped his right hand around the grip in his rage, but he hadn't yet bared the blade. He would doubtless go to that length soon if Eft didn't back off. What, by all the saints, was she doing, anyway? Did it matter at all whether they reached Egypt today or tomorrow or the day after?

Eft assumed her most charming smile—which in a mermaid looks about as friendly as the open arms of an octopus. Her shark's teeth gleamed in the light of the gas lamps. "You are a fool, Captain Calvino, and I will tell you why."

Serafin noticed that the crew members on the bridge pulled their heads a little deeper between their shoulders. They well knew what a storm was going to break over them any moment.

But Calvino was silent, possibly because he was much too flabbergasted. No one had ever dared to speak to him in that tone. His lower lip trembled like the body of an electric eel.

Eft pressed on. "This boat, Captain, was already worth a fortune before the war, more than you and your cutthroats could imagine in your wildest dreams. But today, now that there's no more sea travel, the boat is of such unimaginable worth that not even the treasuries of the suboceanic kingdoms would have been enough for it."

Now she's overdoing it, Serafin thought, but at the same time he saw that Calvino was frowning and listening carefully. Eft was a little closer to her goal: She'd made him curious.

"You've been on board too long, Captain," she continued her harangue, and now the sailors were unmistakably pricking up their ears. "You've forgotten how things look in the world up there. You and your people have let this boat and its art treasures go to ruin while you sail through the world's oceans and look for lost treasure. Yet you'll find the greatest treasure of all here, right under your behind, and you have nothing better to do than turn it into a scrap heap without equal and look on while your crew ruins it a little more day by day."

Calvino's face was still hovering a few inches away from hers, as if frozen in space. "The greatest treasure of all, you say?" Now his voice sounded softer and more controlled than before.

"Certainly—as long as you don't care that it's rotted like an old piece of plank on the shore of some island or other."

"Hmm," said Calvino. "You think I'm . . . untidy?"

"I think," Eft said in a friendly voice, "you are the biggest slob between here and the Arctic Circle, and that in every respect. All the more difficult for me to point out to you your obvious *mistakes*!"

Oh my, oh my, oh my, Serafin thought.

Dario sucked in his breath audibly. "Now she's gone completely crazy," he whispered to his friend.

Captain Calvino stared, wide-eyed, at Eft. His

thumbs nervously polished the pommel of his saber, while his thoughts doubtless circled around murder and manslaughter; around fishwife filet; around a paper-weight made of the jaws of a mermaid.

"Captain?" Eft tilted her head and smiled.

"What?" The word rose growling out of his throat like sulfur vapor from a volcano crater.

"I haven't by any chance offended you, have I?"

Two sailors whispered to each other, and before the two knew it, Calvino was beside them and barking at them with such a gigantic explosion of epithets that even Serafin and Dario, both former street boys from the alleys of Venice, blushed to the tips of their ears.

"Someone should write this down," Dario said out of the side of his mouth.

Calvino started, and his eyes fell on the boys. For a moment it looked as though he was going to let loose his fury on them, too, but then he swallowed his vitupera-tions and turned again to Eft. Dario let go of his breath.

The outburst of rage had calmed the captain a little, and he could now look Eft in the face again without stabbing her with his eyes at the same time. "You are . . . impertinent."

Eft was obviously suppressing a grin, which was prob-ably a good thing, for that is not a beautiful sight in a mer-maid. "This boat is an unparalleled disgrace, Captain. It stinks, it's dirty, and it's neglected. And if I were you—and thanks be to the Lords of the Deep I'm not—I'd make sure that my men brought it into line in a hurry. Every pipe, every picture, every carpet. And then I'd lean back for a moment and enjoy the idea of being one of the richest men in the world."

Serafin watched the words seep into Captain Calvino's consciousness and spread their entire import. One of the richest men in the world. Serafin wondered if Eft knew what she was talking about. On the other hand, you'd have had to be a fool not to recognize what value this submarine had. In times like these it was priceless—if also, and Calvino might overlook that in his greed, *literally* beyond price, for there was no one left who could have bought it.

But presumably the captain would not have sold his boat for any price in the world anyhow. Much more, it was the knowledge of the value of his vessel, the sudden recognition of his wealth, that roused his enthusiasm. He'd been aboard for too long, and as so often happens when one has something around day after day, he'd forgotten how valuable it was.

He looked at Eft for a few seconds longer, then whirled on his heel and snarled a series of orders to his subordinates, who immediately began to relay the captain's wishes to the crew through a speaking tube that reached to the farthest corner of the submarine.

Clean up, the command was. Clean and dust. Remove rust and polish. And then, Calvino ordered, the art treasures that had collected in one of the lower cargo areas over the course of the years should be distributed to the walls and the remaining sound glass cabinets. And woe to him who still dared to do anything to them with charcoal or knife tip!

Finally Calvino gave the former mermaid a crooked grin. "What's your name?"

"Eft."

He bowed gallantly, overdoing it a little, but his good will was evident. "Rinaldo Bonifacio Sergio Romulus Calvino," he introduced himself. "Welcome aboard."

Eft thanked him and then, no longer able to suppress her grin—the captain seemed to be a little frightened by it—she shook his hand and finally went over to the two boys. Serafin and Dario were still standing there with mouths agape, unable to grasp what had just happened.

"How did you do that?" Serafin asked softly as they left the bridge, followed by Calvino's benevolent gaze at Eft's backside.

Eft winked at Serafin. "He's only a man too," she said with satisfaction, "and I still have the eyes of a mermaid."

Then she hurried ahead to supervise the work of cleaning up.

They reached Egypt the next day.

Nothing had prepared them for what they saw as the submarine rose to the surface. Ice floes floated on the open sea, hundreds of yards away from land. The closer they came to the white coastline, the more obvious it became that winter had descended on the desert. No one understood what had happened, and Calvino had his men pray three Our Fathers to protect them all from tritons and sea devils.

Serafin, Eft, and the others were just as mystified as the captain and his crew, and even Lalapeya, the silent, secretive Lalapeya, declared without being asked that she had not the least idea what was going on in Egypt. Without doubt, such an outbreak of winter had never happened before. Ice floes along the desert coast, she explained, were about as usual as polar bears dancing on the tips of the pyramids.

Captain Calvino gave the order to measure the thickness of the ice layer at the bank. Barely more than three feet, it was soon reported to him. Calvino growled ill-humoredly to himself and then conferred with Eft on the bridge for a whole hour—as with every conversation between the two, there was a lot of shouting, terrible curses, and finally a yielding captain.

Shortly afterward Calvino had the boat dive, and they ran into the Nile delta beneath the ice sheet. The great river and its tributaries were not deep, and it required some skill to maneuver the boat between the ice and the river bottom. Sometimes they heard sand grinding under the hull, while the fin-shaped upper projections of the boat's hull scraped along the ice layer. It would be a miracle, raged Calvino, a goddamn miracle if no one noticed them with all this racket.

Most of the time they moved forward at a walking pace, and Serafin began to wonder where they were heading, anyway. The witch's commission had been to set them down on the coast—and now Calvino was voluntarily taking them farther inland, and furthermore, under conditions that were worse than any of them could have imagined. Eft's influence on him was amazing.

The interior of the boat was already gleaming in many places. Everywhere there were sailors busy with cloths and sponges and sandpaper, painting and varnishing, tearing up old carpets and replacing them from the resources of the overflowing storage holds. Many of the stowed objects had lain there for decades, some perhaps since the privateering expeditions of the previous owner, long before the beginning of the mummy war. Even Calvino appeared surprised at what came to light, art treasures and magnificent handwork, such as hadn't been seen for a long time. He became more and more aware, Eft told Serafin, that he'd been imprisoned for too long in the brass world of the submarine and had forgotten to value the beauties of the upper world. Which of course didn't keep him from roaring around like a berserker, screaming at his men, and handing out draconian punishments for overlooked dirt streaks and flakes of rust.

Serafin had a vague feeling that Eft liked the pirate captain. Not the way she'd worshipped Arcimboldo, and yet . . . there was something between the two of them, an absurd love-hate that amused Serafin and at the same time disconcerted him. Was it possible for two people to come closer under such circumstances? Had it been that way with him and Merle? The recognition that they'd spent less time together than Eft and Calvino during the short journey filled his mind. He began to doubt that Merle thought of him as often as he thought of her. Did she miss him? Did he mean anything to her anyway?

A horrible grinding and cracking brought his musings to an abrupt end. It didn't take long before Calvino bellowed out of the speaking tube and, with a string of oaths, informed them of what had happened.

They were stuck. They had run aground in the pack ice of the Nile and could go neither forward nor backward. The iron fins of the submarine had eaten into the ice cover like a saw blade and plowed a lane for a distance of several dozen yards, then became hopelessly wedged in.

Serafin feared the worst and hurried to the bridge. But there stood Calvino and Eft calmly beside each other in front of the windshield of the boat, looking out into the waters of the Nile beneath the ice layer. The witch's fire bubbles had remained back at the coast, but the vague light beams that shimmered through the ice were enough to reveal the most important thing. Through the windshield it looked as if the submarine was stuck under the white ceiling of an indistinct hall. Icicles as thick as tree trunks hung down in front of the window.

It turned out that Captain Calvino was by no means as undisciplined in an emergency as Serafin would have expected. He took account of all the facts, conferred with

Eft, and then gave the order to open the upper hatches of the boat, so that the passengers could climb out.

Climb out? thought Serafin in horror. Had that really been Eft's advice? To simply set them down in the middle of this desert of ice?

An hour later Eft and Lalapeya, Serafin and Dario, Tiziano and Aristide stood ready at the hatch, enveloped in the thickest fur clothing that could be found in the pirates' storage hold. Calvino remembered that the things came from a grounded schooner whose crew he'd annihilated at the beginning of the war. The ship had been on the way to Thule in Greenland, there to load heaven-knew-what in exchange for the warm clothing on board. The jackets, boots, and trousers did not fit any of them—Lalapeya, especially, with her petite body, was at a disadvantage—but they would be enough to protect them from freezing to death. Finally, each put on a shapeless fur cap and slipped both hands into padded mittens. From the weapons room the pirates handed each of them revolvers, ammunition, and knives. Only Lalapeya refused weapons.

Calvino stayed behind with his men to watch the boat and to try to free the top fin from the ice. He thought that it would take many hours, perhaps even days, and the fear of being discovered by the Egyptian sunbarks was clearly written in his face. Although Eft did not ask him to, he promised to wait for three days for a sign of life before he returned to the open sea.

"Where are we going, anyway?" Tiziano morosely said aloud what they'd all wondered a dozen times already.

Eft stood beneath the open hatch that led to the outside. The white circle framed her head like a frozen halo. Her eyes were fixed on Lalapeya, who looked anything but happy in her much-too-large fur clothing. Serafin also inspected the sphinx, and once more he wondered what moved her to keep on accompanying the desperate group. Was it really only hatred for the Empire? The loss of the dead sphinx god who had rested for centuries under the cemetery island of San Michele and whom she had tried in vain to protect from the Empire?

No, thought Serafin, there was something else, something unspoken, which none of them knew anything about. He could feel it as clearly as if the eyes of the sphinx were saying it to him.

"Lalapeya," said Eft. Her words sounded almost festive. "I take it you know where we are. Perhaps you've known the whole time that the first part of our journey would end here."

Lalapeya said nothing, and as much as Serafin tried, he still found no answer in her silence. She confirmed nothing, denied nothing.

Eft went on, "Not far from here, in the middle of the Nile delta, is the fortress of the sphinxes. The mermaids have no name for it, but I think there is one. The captain knows this place, and if the onset of winter has done nothing worse than cover everything with snow and ice, it must be two or three miles from here, at most."

"The Iron Eye sees your living, sees your strivings, sees your dying," Lalapeya recited, and the words sounded to Serafin like a saying from a distant past. The sphinx had passed entire epochs alone in Venice, but she had not forgotten the culture of her people. "The Iron Eye—that's the name you're looking for, Eft. And yes, I can feel it. The closeness of other sphinxes, many in one place. It's suicide to go there." But the way she said it, it didn't sound like a warning but like a confirmation of something that was unavoidable anyway.

"What are we going to do there?" asked Aristide.

"It's the heart of the Empire," said Lalapeya instead of Eft. "If there is a spot where one can injure it, it's there." She said nothing of a plan, perhaps because there was none. The stronghold of the sphinxes, no one doubted, was impregnable.

Eft shrugged, and Serafin thought again about what she had said to the sea witch: that they had to begin somewhere if they wanted to oppose the Empire. That a victory could also lie in small things. Her words had never been out of Serafin's head since then.

But what would it help if they all died doing it? It was as if they were going to run against a wall of their own free will in spite of the certainty that they couldn't even inflict a scratch.

He was just about to give voice to his doubts when he felt Lalapeya gently touch his hand. Without anyone else noticing it, she bent toward his ear and whispered, "Merle is there."

He stared at her, dumbfounded.

Lalapeya smiled.

Merle? he thought, but he didn't dare to put the question. If Dario and the others knew of it, they would accuse him of being involved in this business only because he wanted to see Merle again, not because he believed in their higher goal. *Good,* he thought, *they should follow their higher ideals*; he, anyway, knew why he was *really* doing it, and his motives didn't seem to him any less honorable than theirs. They came out of himself, from his heart.

Lalapeya nodded to him, barely noticeably.

Eft's voice made them both look up at the hatch. Serafin had the feeling he was perceiving everything blurrily, the surroundings, Eft's speech, the presence of the others. Suddenly he was burning to climb up to the outside.

Merle is there, he heard the sphinx say again and again, and the words flitted through his head like moths around a candle.

Eft had not stopped speaking, giving instructions for how to manage in snow, but Serafin scarcely listened.

Merle is there.

At last they set out.

5

BACK TO THE LIGHT

"I CAN FEEL IT. WITH EVERY STEP. EVERY TIME I TAKE A breath." Junipa kept her voice low so no one except Merle could hear her. "It's as if there's something in me . . . here, in my chest . . . something that pulls on me and drags me as if I were on a rope." Her mirror eyes turned to her friend like the signal fire of a lighthouse: silvery light behind glass. "I try to resist it. But I don't know how long I'll be able to do it."

"And you can remember everything that happened in the pyramid?" Merle was holding Junipa's hand and stroking it gently. They were sitting in the farthest corner of the Czarist spies' hiding place.

Junipa swallowed. "I know that I tried to stop you. And that we . . . that we hit each other." She shook her head in shame. "I am so sorry."

"You couldn't help it. It was Burbridge."

"Not him," Junipa contradicted. "The Stone Light. Professor Burbridge is just as much under its control as I am—as long as he's down there, anyway. Then he's not the scientist he used to be anymore, only Lord Light."

"And it's better for you up here?"

Junipa considered for a second before she found the right words. "It feels weaker. Maybe because it's stone and can't penetrate the stone of the Earth's crust. At least not completely. But it isn't gone. It's always with me, all the time. And sometimes it hurts quite a lot."

Merle had seen the scar on Junipa's chest after they climbed out of Hell, the incision through which Burbridge had had a new heart inserted—a splinter of the Stone Light. It was now reposing, cold and motionless, in her chest cavity, keeping her alive as her real heart had done before, like a glowing, sparkling diamond. It healed her wounds in a very short time and lent her strength when she was exhausted. But it also tried to force her under its control.

When Junipa said that it hurt, she didn't mean the pain of the operation, the scar. She meant the pressure to betray Merle another time—the fight against herself, the inner strife between her gentle ego and the icy power of the Stone Light.

And as much as the thought pained Merle, she had to be wary of what Junipa did. It was possible that she'd suddenly stab them in the back a second time.

No, not Junipa, Merle thought bitterly. The Stone Light. The fallen Morning Star in the center of Hell. Lucifer.

She was silent for a moment, and then she spoke about a thing that had been on her mind for a long time. "What you said there, in the pyramid . . ."

"That Burbridge claimed to be your grandfather?"

Merle nodded. "Do you know if that's true?"

"He said it, anyway."

Merle looked at the ground. She opened the buttoned pocket of her dress and pulled out the water mirror, stroking the frame with the tips of her fingers. Her other hand felt for the chicken's foot, now dangling on a cord around her neck, absently playing with the small, sharp claws.

"More soup?" asked a voice behind them.

The two girls turned around. Andrej, the leader of the Czarist spy troop, had sketchily washed the gray color from his face and wore just a part of his mummy armor. He was a tough, grim man, but the presence of the girls brought out a friendliness in him that seemed to amaze his four comrades.

On the other side of the low-ceilinged room, the men were still standing around Vermithrax, their wooden soup bowls in one hand, the other repeatedly stretching toward the obsidian lion's glowing body.

They didn't know that he'd plunged into the Stone Light. In contrast to Junipa, it had gained no power over him. Merle found that strange, but so far she hadn't been able to observe anything disquieting. Since then Vermithrax had been stronger, even a little bigger than before, but aside from his body's lavalike glow, he had not changed. He was the old, good-natured Vermithrax, who now, despite all his concern for his people and his hatred of Seth, was enjoying the admiring attention the Czarists offered him. He basked in their questions, their timid touching, and the respect in their faces. They'd all heard of the stone lions of Venice, even of the few that were able to fly. But that one of those lions was able to speak like a human and, in addition, radiated light like one of the icons in the churches of their homeland—that was new and fascinating to them.

Junipa refused the soup that Andrej offered them, but Merle let him fill her bowl again. After all the days of nourishing herself on tough dried meat, the thin broth seemed like a delicacy to her.

"You do not have to be afraid." Andrej misunderstood the fact that they were sitting in a corner, separated from the others. "The sphinxes will not find us here. We have been here almost six months, and so far they have not once noticed that we exist."

"And you don't find that strange?" Merle asked.

Andrej laughed softly. "We have asked ourselves that a thousand times. The sphinxes are an ancient race, known since the beginning of time to be wise and clever. Do they only observe and tolerate us? Do they feed false information to us? Or are they simply indifferent that we are here because we have no chance of sending our knowledge home anyway?"

"I thought you had carrier pigeons?"

"We did indeed. But how many pigeons can one keep in a place like this before someone notices them? The birds were used up after the first weeks, and there was no way of sending us new ones. Therefore we are only collecting—in our heads, not on paper, nothing is written down—and soon we will return to our homeland. Thanks be to the Baba Yaga."

He gave the girls an encouraging smile, and then he went back to the others. He respected the wish of the two of them to be alone.

"He's strange, don't you think?" said Junipa.

"Very nice," said Merle.

"That too. But so . . . so understanding. Quite different from what you'd expect from someone who secretly traveled halfway around the world and has been hiding in his enemy's stronghold for half a year."

Merle shrugged. "Perhaps his mission has helped him to keep his sanity. He must have seen a lot of bad things." She indicated the other spies with a somber nod. "All of them."

Junipa's eyes wandered from the Czarists over to Seth, who was sitting near the entrance, leaning up against one of the mirror walls. In his bound hands he held a drinking bowl. His ankles were also bound. Had Andrej known who his prisoner really was, he would probably have struck off his head without hesitation. Even if Vermithrax might have agreed thoroughly with that, Merle thought it was wrong. Not because it was unreasonable and quite certainly not because it was undeserved, but she hoped that Seth could still be useful to them. And this time the Flowing Queen shared her opinion.

"Are you going to try it again?" asked Junipa, when she saw Merle's fingertips moving from the frame of the water mirror over the surface.

Merle only nodded and closed her eyes.

Her fingers touched the lukewarm water as if they were lying on glass, without breaking through the faint rings. The murky phantom on the surface brushed against the ends of her fingers. Merle still had her eyes closed, but she could feel him, his frantic rushing back and forth over the water.

She heard his whispers, distorted and much too far away for her to be able to understand them. She must somehow bind the phantom to herself, like a piece of iron to a magnet.

"The word," she whispered to Junipa. "Do you still remember the word?"

"What word?"

"The one Arcimboldo gave us when we had to imprison

the phantoms in the magic mirrors for him." Their old teacher had opened the door through one of his mirrors for them that time in Venice. They had entered the magic mirror world and found the mirror phantoms inside: beings from another world who wanted to cross into this one and then were stranded in Arcimboldo's magic mirrors as spirit-like shadows. The spirits moved almost invisibly and as lightly as wind gusts in the glassy labyrinths of the mirror world, yet they were forever barred from returning or from a further journey into a physical existence. With a magic word the girls had bound them and brought them back to their master, who had let them go into the reflections in the water of the Venetian canals.

"Hmm, the word," murmured Junipa thoughtfully. "Something with *intera* or *intero* at the beginning."

"*Intrabilibus* or something like that."

"Something like it. *Interabilitapetrifax.*"

"*Childish rubbish,*" scolded the Queen.

"*Intrabalibuspustulens,*" said Merle.

"*Interopeterusbilibix.*"

"*Interumpeterfixbilbulus.*"

"*Intorapeterusbiliris.*"

Merle sighed. "*Intorapeti*—wait, say that again!"

"What?"

"What you just said."

Junipa thought for a moment. "*Intorapeterusbiliris.*"

Merle exulted. "Almost! Now I remember:

Intorabiliuspeteris." And she said it so loudly that for a minute even the conversation between the Czarists and Vermithrax on the other side of the room stopped.

"Seth is watching us," Junipa whispered.

But Merle neither bothered about the Horus priest nor paid attention to Junipa's warning. Instead she said the magic word impatiently a second time, and now she suddenly felt a tickling that crept from her right hand up to her elbow.

"Merle!" Junipa's voice became imploring.

Merle blinked and looked at the mirror. The phantom flickered like a circular billow of fog around her fingertips.

"*It worked,*" said the Flowing Queen. She also sounded concerned, as if she were not pleased that Merle was making contact with the phantom.

"Hello?" asked Merle tonelessly.

"Brbrlbrlbrbr!" said the phantom.

"Hello?"

"Harrlll . . . hello."

Merle's heart beat faster with excitement. "Can you hear me?"

Again the strange muttering, then: "Of course. It was you who couldn't hear *me.*" He sounded fresh and not at all ghostly.

"Did he say something?" asked Junipa, and Merle realized that her friend couldn't hear the phantom. Neither could the others in the room, who'd now resumed their conversation and paid no more attention to what Merle was doing. With the exception perhaps of Seth. Yes, he was very definitely observing her. A shudder ran down her back.

"Can you help me?" she asked straightaway. She had no time for verbal sparring. At any moment Andrej could signal them to come for a discussion of their situation.

"I've been wondering when you'd ever get around to that," said the phantom snappishly.

"You will help me?"

He sighed like a mulish little boy. She wondered if that's exactly what he'd been before he became a phantom: a boy, perhaps even still a child. "You want to know what's behind your water mirror, don't you?" he asked.

"Yes."

"Your friend is right. If you call someone who's sometimes a woman and then again a woman with lion's legs a sphinx, then she'd probably be a sphinx."

Merle didn't understand a word. "Could you be a bit clearer?"

Again the phantom sighed. "The woman on the other side is a sphinx. And, yes, she is your mother." When Merle took in her breath sharply, he added, "I think so, anyhow. Now are you satisfied?"

"What's he saying?" whispered Junipa excitedly. "Tell me!"

Merle's heart was racing. "He said the sphinx is my mother!"

"He said the sphinx is my mother," the phantom

mimicked, mocking her. "Now, do you want to know more, or not?"

"*He is an ill-bred brat,*" commented the Flowing Queen. The phantom didn't seem to be able to hear her, for he didn't react to that.

"Yes," said Merle, her voice wobbling, "yes, of course. Where is she now? Can you see her?"

"No. She doesn't have a wonderful mirror like the one in which you're holding me prisoner."

"Holding you prisoner? You jumped into it yourself!"

"Because otherwise the same thing would have happened to me as the others."

"Did you know them?"

"They were all from my world. But I only knew my uncle. He didn't want me to come with him, but then I sneaked into his workroom at night and jumped into the mirror after him. He looked really dumb when he noticed it." The phantom giggled. "Oh, well, and then *I* looked dumb when I realized what had happened to us."

"*Jawing,*" the Queen said, "*nothing but jawing.*"

"Let's talk about my mother again, all right?"

"Sure," said the phantom. "Whatever you want."

"Where is she now?"

"The last time I saw her she was sitting on a dead witch in the middle of the sea." He said it as matter-of-factly as if he'd seen her cooking.

"In the sea?" Merle asked. "Are you sure?"

"I *know* how the sea looks," he replied spitefully.

"Yes . . . yes, sure. But, I mean, what was she doing there?"

"Holding one hand in the water and creating a magic mirror out of it. So she could hold your hand. Remember?"

Merle was terribly confused. "So can you only see her when she holds one hand in the water?"

"Just like you."

"And you hear her too?"

"Both of you."

"But then why can't I hear her?"

"We could change places anytime," he retorted snippily.

Merle thought for a while. "You must tell me what she says. Does she know how to speak with you?"

"She very quickly tumbled to the fact that there's someone in the mirror besides her little daughter. And she was polite enough to ask me my name first."

"Oh . . . what's your name, then?"

"I've forgotten."

"But how—"

"I said that she asked, not that I could give her an answer."

"How can anyone forget his name?"

"How can anyone suddenly become a dust mark on a mirror? No idea. The only thing I can remember are the last few seconds in my uncle's room. Everything before that is gone. But I have the feeling that it's gradually coming back. Sometimes I remember details, faces, even tunes. Perhaps if you carry me around for a few more years in your musty pocket, then—"

This time it was she who interrupted him. "Listen. I'm sorry about what happened to you, but I can't do anything about it. No one forced you to run after your uncle. So—do you intend to help me or not?"

"Yes, yes, yes," he said, drawling.

"If you can talk with"—Merle hesitated—"my mother, then you can pass on to her what I say. And the other way around."

"A sort of translation, you mean?"

"Exactly." Now he's got it, she thought, and even the Queen sighed somewhere deep in her thoughts.

"Guess I could probably do that."

"That would be very nice."

"Then will you take me out of your pocket sometimes?"

"If we ever get away from here in one piece, we might find a way to get you out of this mirror."

"*Do not be too generous with promises you may not be able to keep,*" said the Queen.

"That won't happen." The phantom sounded a little sad. "I can't take on a body in your world. Everyone said that."

"Maybe not a body. But a larger mirror. How about the sea?"

"Then I'd be something like a sailor, wouldn't I?"

"I suppose."

"Hmm . . . I guess that would be all right." And then he began to sing a song, quite tunelessly, something about fifteen men on a dead man's chest. Quite nonsensical, Merle thought.

"We'll try," she said hastily, so that he'd stop the howling. "Promise."

"Merle?" Suddenly he sounded serious.

"Yes?"

"Merle . . ."

She was breathing faster. "What is it?"

"She's here again. Your mother, Merle . . . she's here with me."

"What the devil is she doing?" Dario shifted crossly from one foot to the other. The snow crunched under the soles of his boots, and Serafin thought that Dario's teeth would soon crunch just as much, from fury, if Lalapeya didn't stand up that instant and go on.

The sphinx was crouching on the bank of the frozen Nile, between blocks of fractured ice whose edges had shoved over and under one another. The boys had taken shelter in a dead palm grove only a few yards away. The palm fronds had long since broken off under the burden of snow, and all that remained were just a few slanting trunks sticking out of the white wasteland like fingers. The boys among the dead trees made splendid targets from the air. Eft was not with them; she stood below on the bank beside the sphinx, looking down at her worriedly.

Serafin couldn't stand it any longer. "I'm going down to them."

He looked at the Iron Eye one more time; it rose above them like a gray wall, an incomprehensibly high monstrosity. You could have taken it for a mountain, if it hadn't risen so smoothly and abruptly out of the icy plain. The twilight helped to veil the true nature of the fortress.

Somewhere behind the snow clouds the sun was going down. At least they soon wouldn't need to fear the barks any longer. But certainly there were other guards outside, here at the foot of the Iron Eye. Guards who were still fast and deadly at night.

Dario murmured something as Serafin clomped away, but he made no move to follow him. That was quite all right with Serafin. He wanted to speak with Eft and the sphinx alone.

But when he finally looked over Lalapeya's shoulder and saw what she was doing, the words remained stuck in his throat.

A hole gaped in the ice at the water's edge. It looked as if a predator had scratched it with its claws. So close to the Iron Eye, the ice was much thinner than the place where the boat had gotten stuck. Twelve inches, Serafin estimated, at most. That must be because of the warmth radiating from the fortress. It had certainly become warmer, but the temperature was still way below freezing.

Lalapeya was crouching in the snow, bent forward, her arm plunged into the water up to the elbow. Her hand was motionless in the ice-cold stream. The sphinx had shoved back the sleeve of her fur coat; her naked lower arm was slowly turning blue. Nevertheless she made no move to withdraw the hand. Only now did Serafin notice that she was whispering something to herself. Too softly. He couldn't understand what she was saying.

Distressed, he turned to Eft, who'd stepped up beside him. "What's she doing?"

"She's speaking with someone."

"Her hand will freeze."

"It probably already has."

"But—"

"She knows what she's doing."

"No," he said angrily, "obviously she doesn't! We can't burden ourselves with dragging her into the fortress half-frozen." He reached out his hand to pull Lalapeya back by the shoulder, away from the water.

But Eft halted him, and the hissing that suddenly came from her shark mouth made him flinch. "It's important. Really important."

Serafin staggered back a step. "She's crazy. Both of you are crazy." He was about to turn away and go back to the others. But again Eft held him back.

"Serafin," said the mermaid imploringly, "she's speaking with Merle."

He stared at her dumbfounded. "What do you mean?"

"The water helps her do it." Eft waved Serafin a few steps farther away and there—on the bank of the frozen Nile—Serafin now learned what was special about Merle's water mirror.

He folded his arms over his chest and rubbed his upper arms under the fur, more from nervousness than from cold. "Is that the truth?" he asked with a frown. "I mean, are you really serious?"

Eft nodded.

Serafin lowered his voice. "But what does Merle have to do with Lalapeya?"

The mermaid showed her teeth: a smile. "Can't you figure that out?"

"No, damn it!"

"She's her mother, Serafin. Lalapeya is Merle's mother." Her fearsome grin grew wider, but her eyes remained human and wondrously beautiful. "Your friend is the daughter of a sphinx."

Merle listened with concentration to the phantom's words while at the same time she struggled not to let her trembling fingers dip too far into the reflection. She mustn't let the connection to him break off now, she had to hear what the sphinx—her mother—had to say to her.

"She says you must go to Boerbritch," the phantom repeated.

"Burbridge?" Merle asked.

"You should go to him, only there are you safe. Safer anyway than in the Iron Eye."

"But we just got away from Burbridge, out of Hell! Tell her that."

A while passed, then the phantom brought back the answer. "She wants me to tell you that you should meet him in his mirror room. You and your friend. She should guide you there."

"Junipa guide me into a mirror room?"

"Yes. Wait, that's not all . . . ah, now. She should take you to him. There you will be safe."

Merle still didn't understand. "Safe from whom? From the sphinxes?"

Again a pause, then: "From the Son of the Mother, she says. Whatever that means."

Merle growled in annoyance. "Would you be so good as to *ask*?"

While the phantom obeyed, the Queen chimed in. *"I do not know if that is such a good idea, Merle. Perhaps you should—"*

No, Merle thought decidedly. You stay out of this. This is my affair alone.

The voice of the phantom reported back. "The Son of the Mother. That seems to be something like a name for . . . yes, *the* forefather of the sphinxes, as it were, their oldest ancestor. A kind of sphinx god, I guess. She says he is on the way here, or is even in the fortress. She is not sure. And she says that the sphinxes are going to try to awaken him to life again."

Merle was startled when the Queen uttered a strange sound. How much do you know, really? she thought for the hundredth time.

"The Son of the Mother," whispered the Queen. *"Then it is true. I felt him but I thought it was impossible. . . . By all that is holy, Merle, you must not do what she asks. You must not go away from here."*

You could have told me about that before, Merle thought bitterly. You ought to have trusted me.

The phantom went on, "She keeps saying the same thing, Merle. That your friend must take you to Burbridge, before it's too late. That you should go into his mirror room and should wait there for him if necessary. She says he can explain everything to you, about you, about her, and about your father."

"Ask her who my father was."

The pause grew longer. "Burbridge's son," said the phantom finally. "Steven."

Steven Burbridge. Her father. The thought felt strange and frightened her.

"What is her name?"

"Lalapeya," said the phantom.

Merle felt her fingers begin to tremble. She bit her lips and tried to pull herself together. It was all so confusing and so overwhelming at the same time. Had the sphinxes not been her enemies from the beginning? Were they not the true rulers of the Empire? If her mother was actually a sphinx, then her people had plunged the world into ruin. But Merle was not like them, and perhaps Lalapeya wasn't either.

"Merle," the phantom interrupted her train of thought, "your mother says that only Junipa can guide you. That is very important. Only Junipa has the power to use the glass word."

Merle was as dizzy as if she'd been whirling in a circle for hours. "The glass word? What's that supposed to be?"

"One moment."

Time passed. Much too much time.

"Hello?" she asked after a while.

"She's gone."

"What?"

"Lalapeya took her hand out of the water. I can't hear her anymore."

"But that's—"

"Sorry. Not my fault."

Merle looked up and for the first time was aware of Junipa again, who sat in front of her, filled with concern. "I should guide you? He said that?"

Merle nodded, numb, as after a nightmare. She ought to have been celebrating. Now she knew who her parents were. But it changed so little. Really, nothing at all. It only confused her even more, and it frightened her.

In a whisper, she told Junipa everything. Then she looked up and saw that Seth had not taken his eyes off them. He smiled icily when their eyes met. She quickly looked away.

"I know what he meant," Junipa whispered tonelessly.

"Really?"

Junipa was breathing shallowly, her voice sounded hoarse. "Through the mirrors, Merle. We should go through the mirrors." She smiled sadly. "That's what Arcimboldo gave me these eyes for, after all, isn't it? I can not only *see* with them. They're also a key, or at least a part of one. Burbridge told me everything: why he gave Arcimboldo the commission to take me out of the orphanage and so forth. I was supposed to look into other worlds, but I can also go there."

"Even back to Burbridge?" Merle whispered. "Back to Lord Light?"

Junipa's smile seemed even more downcast, but somewhere in the gleam and glitter of her eyes was also something else: a faint, shy triumph.

"Everywhere," she said.

"But why—"

"Why didn't we do that long ago? Because it isn't so

simple. I need something for it, the same thing with which Arcimboldo opened the door in the mirror that time in the workshop."

Merle saw the scene flash before her: Arcimboldo, as he bent before the mirror and moved his lips. How he soundlessly formed a word.

"The glass word," said Junipa, as she let the sound of the syllables melt on her tongue. "I didn't know they called it that."

"And you don't know how it sounds?"

"No," Junipa said. "Arcimboldo was murdered before he could tell me."

Good God, Serafin thought, when Lalapeya pulled her right hand out of the water. It was gray up to the wrist, almost blue, and looked as if it were made of wax. It hung at the end of her arm as if it no longer belonged to her body. Lifeless, as if it were dead.

The sphinx's features were twisted with pain, but still the fire of her willpower burned in her fawn-colored eyes.

"Eft," she said, paying no attention to Serafin.

Eft quickly bent toward her and was about to help Lalapeya to stand, but she'd misunderstood the sphinx: Lalapeya was not asking for help.

"Merle needs . . . the word," she said doggedly.

Eft shook her head. "We must look after your hand. If we could somehow manage a fire—"

"No." Lalapeya looked pleadingly at Eft. "First the word."

"What does she mean?" asked Serafin.

"Please!" The sphinx sounded tearful.

Serafin's eyes fastened on Eft. "What word?"

"The glass word." Eft looked at the ground, past Lalapeya, as if she saw something in front of her in the snow. But there was only a shadow there, and she stared at it as if she were asking for advice.

"Merle and Junipa must go to Burbridge," said Lalapeya. "Junipa has the *sight*, she is a guide. But to open the door, the door of mirror glass, she needs the glass word." The sphinx held her deadened hand pressed firmly to her chest with her healthy left one. Serafin had never had frostbite himself, but he'd heard that it was just as painful as being burned. It was astonishing that Lalapeya didn't collapse.

"I don't know the word," said Eft hesitantly.

"You, no. But he."

Serafin stared at the two women, his eyes wide. "He?" And then he understood. "Arcimboldo?"

Lalapeya didn't answer, but Eft nodded slowly.

"Merle has a right to the truth. I don't have enough strength . . . to tell her everything. Not here." Lalapeya looked down at her inert, waxy right hand. "But the word . . . that I can tell her." Her gaze became entreating. "Right now, Eft!"

Eft hesitated a moment longer, and Serafin, who felt terribly helpless in his ignorance, would have liked to have taken her by the shoulders and shaken her: Do it now! Do something! Help her!

Eft sighed deeply, then nodded. Swiftly she loosened her knapsack and pulled out the mirror mask: a perfect replica of Arcimboldo's features in silvery mirror glass. Eft had made it after the mirror maker's death, and Serafin had the dark suspicion that this was Arcimboldo's real face, taken from the corpse and changed by mysterious magic into glass.

Eft handed the mask to Lalapeya.

"Will he speak with me?" the sphinx asked doubtfully.

"With anyone who puts it on."

Serafin looked from one to the other. He didn't dare disturb them with questions.

Lalapeya regarded the wrinkled features of the mirror master for a few seconds, then turned the mask and inspected the inside. Uncertainty flashed in her eyes for a moment, then she pressed the glass to her face with her left hand. The mask remained stuck, even though she took her hand away. The interior seemed in some miraculous way to fit Lalapeya's narrow features; the glass fitted over her face without overhanging the sides.

Serafin watched breathlessly, almost expecting to hear Arcimboldo's voice speak. He felt distaste for the idea; it seemed to him undignified, like the tired old tricks of a ventriloquist.

A minute passed, during which none of them moved. Even those left behind in the palm grove were silent, although they couldn't see exactly what was going on in front of them. Serafin guessed that the boys felt it anyway, just as he did himself. One could feel the magic, which radiated in all directions through the ice and cold, perhaps even into the river, where it induced the fins of the frozen fish cadavers to flutter. The hairs on the backs of Serafin's hands were standing up, and for the same reason he felt a gentle pressure behind his eyeballs, as with a bad cold. But the feeling passed as quickly as it had come.

Lalapeya placed her sound hand over the mask with fingers spread and effortlessly pulled it off. Underneath, her face was unscathed, not even reddened. Eft sighed when the sphinx returned her glassy mirror shell to her.

"That was all?" asked Serafin.

Eft shoved the mask back into her knapsack. "You wouldn't say that if *you* had had it on your face."

Lalapeya bent over the opening in the ice again.

"No," whispered Serafin. But he didn't hold her back. They all knew that it was the only way.

Lalapeya plunged her sound left hand into the water. Serafin thought he could feel the cold creeping up it, the blood leaving her lower arm, and the skin turning white. Sphinxes were creatures of the desert, and the icy cold must hurt her terribly.

Again minutes passed in which nothing moved, in which the frost itself held its breath around them and the icy wind came to a standstill over the plain. Lalapeya's face grew paler and paler while she exposed her hand to the cold and the flesh gradually went dead. But she didn't pull it back; she waited patiently and felt under the ice in the darkness for an answer to her silent call.

Then the corner of her mouth twitched: the fleeting shadow of a smile. Her eyelids closed as in a deep, deep dream.

She whispered.

A tear flowed from the corner of her eye and turned to ice.

"What sort of a word is *that* supposed to be?" yelped the phantom.

"Magic words are always tongue twisters," Merle explained. "Most of them, anyway." She said it as convincingly as if she had actually heard more than two of them in her life.

The phantom grew more heated. "But such a word!" He had needed five attempts before he was certain that he had said it right, just as Lalapeya had said it to him on the other side.

Merle had to confess that she still couldn't keep it in her head. Compared to that, she spoke the magic word for the mirror phantoms as easily as a nursery rhyme.

But Junipa nodded and that was the main thing. "I can say it. It's quite simple." She said it, and it sounded perfect.

She *is* a guide, thought Merle, impressed and at the same time a little disturbed. Whatever it might mean—she actually was one!

"Tell my mother—," she began, but the phantom interrupted her.

"She's gone again."

"Oh."

For the first time the phantom sounded as if he felt a little pity for Merle's situation. "Don't be sad," he said gently. "She'll be back again. Most certainly. This business was quite . . . difficult for her."

"What exactly do you mean by difficult?"

"You'll worry yourself unnecessarily."

If the phantom had intended to soothe Merle with that, he achieved exactly the opposite. "What's wrong with her? Is she sick? Or injured?" she asked in alarm.

So the phantom told her what Lalapeya had undergone in order to produce the contact. And that she thus might lose both her hands.

Merle pulled her fingers back and let the mirror sink. For a moment she stared into emptiness.

Now she no longer doubted that the sphinx was her mother.

"Merle?"

She looked up.

Junipa smiled encouragingly. "Do you want to try it? I mean, right now?"

Merle took a deep breath and looked around at the others. The spies were still standing beside Vermithrax. He was telling them in his full-toned lion's voice about their adventures in Hell. At another time Merle would perhaps have been concerned that he was telling too much—especially as Seth was listening intently from his corner—but at the moment she had other things on her mind.

"Can you do it, then?" she asked Junipa. "Here?"

Junipa nodded. Merle followed her eyes to the mirrored wall and saw her own reflection crouching depressed on the floor, her fist clenching the handle of the water mirror.

"The mirrors," she whispered, shoving the water mirror into her pocket and buttoning it and touching the ice-cold wall with her other hand. "That's it, isn't it? That's why everything is made of mirrors here. The sphinxes have made a doorway. They want to pull down the walls between the worlds with their fortress. First they conquer this world, and then the next, and then another and—" She broke off as she realized that this was the same plan the Stone Light was following. Where was the connection? There must be a connecting link between the sphinxes and the Light.

"*Let it be,*" said the Flowing Queen. Merle had almost

forgotten her, she'd been so silent during the past few hours. *"What if you do not like the answer?"*

Merle had no time to think over the Queen's words. Junipa had stood up and extended her hand in invitation.

"Come," she said.

On the other side of the room, Seth raised an eyebrow. Andrej also looked at them. Merle smiled at him.

"I can stop you," said the Queen.

"No," Merle said, and knew that it was the truth.

Then, hand in hand with Junipa, she stepped in front of the wall. She saw the reflections of the men, saw how they all turned around in amazement.

Junipa whispered the glass word.

They entered the mirror, plunging wonderingly into a sea of silver.

6

HER TRUE NAME

MIRRORS AND MIRRORS AND MIRRORS. A WHOLE WORLD
of them.

A world among the mirrors. Behind them, between
them, beside them. Lanes and tunnels, all of silver.
Reflections of reflections of themselves.

And right in the middle of it: thousands of Merles,
thousands of Junipas.

"As if we were traveling back through time," said
Merle.

Junipa didn't let go of her hand, leading her like a child
through the strange environment. "What do you mean?"

"How long has it been since Arcimboldo sent us behind the mirror to catch the phantoms?"

"I don't know. It seems to me as—"

"As if it were years, right?"

"An eternity."

"That's what I mean," Merle said. "When we go back to Venice—and someday we will do that, won't we?—so, when we go back to Venice, a lot of things there will probably be different. Almost certainly. But here, nothing has changed at all. Only mirrors, mirrors, mirrors."

Junipa nodded slowly. "But no phantoms."

"No phantoms," Merle confirmed.

"At least, not here."

"Is the mirror world actually its own world?" Merle asked.

"It's more a place in the midst of all the other worlds. Or better, sort of a saucer with many worlds lying around it, like the universe around the planets. You have to go through the saucer to get into the next world. Arcimboldo explained it to me, but he also said that it would take many years to grasp only a fraction of it. Longer than one life. Or many lives. And Burbridge thinks this is too big for the comprehension of a human being. 'Too little, really,' he said."

"Too little, really," the Queen repeated in Merle's thoughts. Was she of the same opinion? Or did she see everything quite differently? As she had so often in recent days, she remained silent.

Merle thought about Vermithrax, whom she'd left behind on the other side of the mirror. The obsidian lion would certainly be terribly concerned about her. We should have let him in on it, she thought. We ought to have told him what we were going to do. But how would they have done that without letting Seth and the Czarists know about it?

Poor Vermithrax.

"He knows you," said the Flowing Queen. *"He knows that you will come through somehow. Better worry about yourself instead of him."*

Merle was about to contradict her when the Queen added, *"And if you are only worrying about Vermithrax, he will reproach himself for the rest of his life if something happens to you."*

That's mean, she thought angrily. And terribly unfair.

But the Queen had already subsided into her brooding silence again.

The girls went farther through the labyrinth of mirrors, crisscross, in a crazy zigzag, and the longer they were under way, the more Junipa blossomed. Over and over again, where Merle expected a pathway, there was only a new wall of glass and another one to the right of it and to the left of it, but nevertheless, Junipa found the narrowest crack between them, the loophole, the needle eye in this glittering, flashing, sparkling infinity.

"The sphinxes must have been here," said Merle.

"Do you really think so?"

"Just look around. The Iron Eye is a replica. Mirrors everywhere, reflecting themselves. Over and over, reflecting oneself to oneself. The Iron Eye is a copy of this, a reflection of the mirror world, as it were. Only much clearer, much . . . *more rational*. Here everything appears to be so random. If I go to the right, am I really going to the right? And is left actually left? Where's up and down and front and back?" She was going to stop at what she thought was a dead end in front of her, but Junipa pulled her on, and they passed the place without encountering any resistance. To Junipa, the path appeared to be obvious, as if her mirror eyes had picked out a pathway. To Merle it was a miracle.

She regarded her friend from the side, letting her eyes slide over the girl's delicate profile, the sweep of her milky-white skin. She stopped at the mirror shards in her eyes.

"What do you see?" she asked. "I mean, *here* . . . how do you know the right way?"

Junipa smiled. "I just see it. I don't know how to explain it. It's as if I'd already been here before. When you go through Venice, you know the way too, without having to look for particular spots, for signposts or things like that. You simply go and eventually you get there. By yourself. It's the same thing for me here."

"But you were never here before."

"No, I wasn't. But maybe my eyes were."

She was silent for a while until Merle took up the conversation again. "Are you angry at Arcimboldo?"

"Angry?" Junipa laughed brightly, and it sounded sincere. "How could I be angry at him? I was blind and he gave me sight."

"But he did it on Lord Light's orders."

"Yes and no. Lord Light, Burbridge . . . he ordered Arcimboldo to take us out of the orphanages. And the business with the eyes was also his idea. But that isn't the only reason Arcimboldo did it. He wanted to help me. The two of us."

"Without him we wouldn't be here."

"Without him the Flowing Queen would be a prisoner of the Egyptians or dead. Just like us and the rest of Venice. Have you ever considered it from that angle?"

Merle was of the opinion that she had regarded it from every possible angle. Naturally they were only free because Arcimboldo had taken them to be his apprentices. But what was this freedom worth? Basically they were prisoners like all the others—worse, even, they were prisoners of a fate that left them no choice except the way they had taken. It would have been so comfortable to stop, lean back, and say to themselves that someone else would settle the whole thing. But that wasn't the way things were. The responsibility was theirs alone.

She wondered if Arcimboldo had possibly foreseen

this. And if that was why he'd engaged in the trading with Lord Light.

"We'll be there soon," said Junipa.

"So fast?"

"You can't measure the paths here with our measures. Each of them is a shortcut in its own way. That's the point of the mirror world: to get quickly from one place to another."

Merle nodded, and suddenly she had the feeling that everything Junipa was telling her wasn't so weird at all. The more fantastic the things on her trip had turned out to be, the less astonishing they seemed to Merle. She couldn't help wondering how long ago it had been. When had the old world come apart for her and turned into something new? It wasn't at the moment when the Queen entered into her, but yet it was that same night, when she said good-bye to the old Merle for the first time and opened the door to the new one; when she'd left the festival with Serafin and let herself fall into that completely unlooked-for moment; when she'd become a little more comfortable with the idea of being grown up soon.

"There it is," said Junipa. "In front of us."

Merle blinked, saw only herself in the mirror at first, and thought acidly that it was the perfect reflection of her brooding: always only herself, herself, herself.

"*Your self-pity is so unbearable sometimes,*" the Flowing Queen said. And after a pause she asked, "*Don't you have a smart answer?*"

You're really right.

Junipa grasped her hand more firmly and pointed to a spot in the silvery infinity. "That's the door."

"Oh, really?"

"Does that mean you can't see it?"

"Someone forgot to screw on the doorknob."

Junipa smiled. "Just trust me."

"I do that all the time."

Junipa stopped and turned to her. "Merle?"

"Um?"

"I'm glad you're here. That we're going through this business together."

Merle smiled. "Now you sound entirely different from before, in the Iron Eye. Much more . . . like yourself."

"Here between the mirrors I can't feel the Stone Light anymore," said Junipa. "It's as if I had an entirely normal heart. And I can see better than you or probably anyone else. I think I belong here."

And perhaps that was the truth; perhaps Arcimboldo had in fact created her eyes out of the glass of the mirror world. *Junipa is a guide,* Lalapeya had said. And weren't guides always natives of the place? The thought sent shivers down Merle's spine, but she made an effort not to show it.

"Don't let go of my hand," said Junipa. Then she whispered the glass word tonelessly and the two of them took the decisive step together.

Leaving the mirror world was accomplished just as unspectacularly as entering it. They went through the glass as if they were passing through a soft breeze, and on the other side they found—

"Mirrors?" Merle asked before she realized that this was by no means the same place from which they'd started.

"*Mirrors?*" the Flowing Queen asked as well.

"Burbridge's mirror room," said Junipa. "Exactly as your mother said."

Behind them someone cleared his throat. "I'd hoped you'd find the way here."

Merle whirled around, even faster than Junipa.

Professor Burbridge, Lord Light, her grandfather—three completely different meanings in one person. He walked up to them but stopped a few steps away. He didn't come too close, as if he didn't want to make them nervous.

"Don't worry," he said. "In here I'm only myself. The Light has no power over me in the mirror room." He sounded older than outside in Hell. And he looked that way too: He was much more bent now, and he acted frail.

"In this place I am not Lord Light," he said with a sad smile. "Still only Burbridge, the old fool."

The mirror out of which they'd walked was only one of many, arranged in a wide circle. Most were still in the glued frames that Arcimboldo had placed around the magic mirrors when he supplied them to his customers.

The mirrors that Arcimboldo had sold to Lord Light were arranged on the walls, maybe a hundred, maybe two hundred of them. Some were also lying on the floor like puddles of quicksilver, others hung flat beneath the ceiling.

"They keep the Stone Light away from here," Burbridge explained. He wore a morning coat similar to the one he'd had on at their first meeting. His hair was disheveled and he looked untidy, as if his dapper appearance before was only a semblance that the Stone Light had kept in place. All that faded in here. The pouches under his eyes were heavier, his eyes lay deeper in their sockets. The veins showed dark on the parchmentlike backs of his hands. Liver spots covered his skin like the shadows of insects.

"We're alone." He'd noticed that Merle kept surveying the room mistrustfully, for fear of the Lilim, Burbridge's creatures. He appeared to be telling the truth, in fact.

"My mother sent me." Suddenly it didn't feel at all difficult to use that word. It sounded almost matter-of-fact: *my mother.*

Burbridge raised an eyebrow in surprise. "Lalapeya? How I hated her in the old days. And she me, no doubt about that. And now she's sending you here, of all places?"

"She said you could explain everything to me. The truth about me and my parents. About Lalapeya . . . and about Steven."

Burbridge had been standing in the center of the room at her arrival, as if he'd expected her coming.

"*It is because of the mirrors,*" the Flowing Queen said. "*If the mirrors really protect him, then perhaps he is safest in the center where their looks meet.*" Arcimboldo had said something similar to her once: "Look into a mirror, and it looks back at you. Mirrors can see!"

"*It is no coincidence,*" the Queen continued, "*that Burbridge named the capital city of Hell Axis Mundi, the axis of the world. The same way that symbolically marks the center point of Hell, this place here is the axis of his existence, his own center, the place where he is still always himself, without the influence of the Light.*" After a short pause, she added, "*Most are on the search for their center their entire life long, for the axis of their world, but only the fewest are aware of it.*"

Burbridge again took two steps in the girls' direction. The movement had nothing threatening about it.

Is *he* my axis? Merle asked in her thoughts. My center?

The Queen laughed softly. "*He? Oh, no. But the center is often that which stands at the end of our search. You have sought your parents, and you are perhaps on the point of finding them. Perhaps your family is your center, Merle. And Burbridge is, for good or evil, a part of it. But sometime you will perhaps seek other things.*"

Then is the center something like that happiness that one always seeks but never finds?

"*It can be happiness, but also your downfall. Some seek their entire lives for nothing but death.*"

At least they can be certain that they'll find it some-time, Merle thought.

"Do not joke about it. Look at Burbridge! The Stone Light has kept him alive for decades. Do you not think he is ready for death? And if he will find it anywhere, it will be here, where the Light cannot get at him. At least not yet."

Not yet?

"The Light will know of our presence. And it will not look on much longer without taking action in spite of all this."

Then we must hurry.

"Good idea."

Merle turned to Burbridge. "I must learn the truth. Lalapeya says it's important."

"For her or for you?" The old man seemed amused and at the same time desperately sad.

"Will you tell me about it?"

His eyes slid over the endless round of mirrors. Arcimboldo's legacy. "You perhaps don't know much about Lalapeya," he said. "Only that she is a sphinx, isn't that so?"

Merle nodded.

"There is also a piece of the Stone Light in Lalapeya, Merle. As in you yourself, for you are her child. But I'll get to that. First the beginning, yes? Always the begin-ning first . . . A long time ago the sphinx Lalapeya received the task of protecting a grave. Not just any grave, it goes without saying, but the grave of the first ancestor of all the sphinxes. Their progenitor and not, as many believe, their god—although he easily could become that, if his old power awakens again. They call him the Son of the Mother. After his death thousands upon thousands of years ago, the sphinx people laid him to rest in a place that later was to become the lagoon of Venice. At that time there was nothing, only gloomy swamps, into which no living thing strayed. They set watchers, a long line of watchers, and the last of them was Lalapeya. In that time, during Lalapeya's watch, it happened that men settled in the lagoon, first building simple huts, then houses, and finally, over the course of the centuries, an entire city."

"Venice."

"Quite right. The sphinxes ordinarily avoided humans; in fact, they outright hated them, but Lalapeya differed from the others of her people, and she decided to leave the men and women alone. She admired their strong wills and their determination to wrest a new home from the wet, desolate wasteland."

An axis, thought Merle in sudden comprehension. A center of their small, sorrowful human world. And the Queen said, "It is so."

"Over the centuries the lagoon took on the form that you know today, and Lalapeya abided there all that time. Finally she was living in a palazzo in the Cannaregio district. And there my son met her. Steven."

"Who was Steven's mother?"

"A Lilim. Naturally not one like the ones you've come to know. Not one of those barbaric beasts, and not a plump shape changer, either. She was what people in the upper world call a succubus. A Lilim in the shape of a wonderfully beautiful woman. And she *was* beautiful, believe me. Steven grew into a child who carried the inheritance of both parents in him, mine as well as hers."

This thought made Merle's head spin. Her mother was a sphinx, her father half human, half Lilim. What was she herself, then?

"I often brought Steven here as a child," said Burbridge. "I told him of the Stone Light, what it was doing to us, what it was making of us. Even then, as a little boy, he resisted this idea. And when he was older, he went away. He told no one of it, not even me. He took a secret gateway, which ended in the lagoon, and he felt the influence of the Light fall away from him. He must have thought he could live as a quite normal human being." Burbridge lowered his voice. "I myself had lost this dream a long, long time ago. When I was still able to flee, I didn't want to. And today I cannot. The Light would not permit it. Steven, on the other hand, was unimportant to it, yes, perhaps it was even glad that he was gone—always provided that it thinks at all like a human, of which I have some doubt.

"So Steven went to Venice and remained there. He met

Lalapeya, perhaps by chance, although I rather believe that she sensed where he came from. He was, like her, a stranger in the city, a stranger among your people. And for a while they were together."

"Why didn't they stay together?"

"What neither had thought possible happened. Lalapeya became pregnant and brought you into the world, Merle. Steven . . . well, he went away."

"But why?"

"You must know him to understand that. He couldn't bear it when anyone held him fast anywhere, when anyone subjected him to firm . . . firm obligations. I don't know how to express it. It was the same as in Hell. He hated the Stone Light because it rules us all and only rarely allows one's own thoughts. He felt himself constricted again by Lalapeya and her child, again limited in his freedom. And I think that was the reason he went away."

Merle's lower lip trembled. "What a coward!"

Burbridge hesitated a moment before he answered. "Yes, perhaps he is one. Just a coward. Or a rebel. Or a disastrous mixture of both. But he is also my son and your father, and we should not pass judgment on him hastily."

Merle saw it entirely differently, but she remained silent so that Burbridge would tell her the rest. "Lalapeya was in despair. She had detested me from the beginning. Steven had told her everything about the Light and about my role in the world of the Lilim. Lalapeya blamed me for

Steven's disappearance. In her anger and her grief she wanted nothing more to do with Steven, and also not with her child, in whom she saw a piece of Steven."

Junipa grasped Merle's hand.

"Is that why she put me out on the canal?"

Burbridge nodded. "I think she's regretted it many times. But she hadn't the strength to make herself known to her daughter. She was still always the watcher of the forefather, the Son of the Mother."

Merle thought of the water mirror, of the many times when she'd pushed her hand in and was touched by the fingers on the other side. Always tenderly, always full of warmth and friendship. It didn't go with what Burbridge said: Lalapeya had made herself known to her, even if in the unique, mysterious way of a sphinx.

"Lalapeya must have known that you were living in the orphanage. Probably she was observing your every step," Burbridge went on. "It was harder for me. It took years, but finally Arcimboldo located you on my orders and took you to him." His eyes sought Junipa and found her half-hidden behind Merle. "Just like you, Junipa. Even if for other reasons."

Junipa made a face. "You made me into a slave. So that I could spy on other worlds for the Stone Light."

"Yes," he said sadly, "that too. That was *one* reason, but it wasn't mine; rather, it was the Light's. I myself wanted something different."

Merle's voice became icy when she understood. "He used you, Junipa. Not for himself, but for me. He wanted you to bring me here. That was the reason, right, Professor? You had the eyes put into her so that she could show me the way to the mirror room."

Again Burbridge nodded, visibly affected. "I couldn't have you brought here by the Lilim—that would only have made the Light aware of you. When you finally came into Hell of your own free will with the lion, you were in the kingdom of the Light. And how little power I possess there you have already seen, when the Lilim took you prisoner. I wanted to spare you all that. Junipa was to have brought you here through the mirrors, as she did today, into this room, where you are safe from the influence of the Light." He paused a moment and wiped his forehead. Then he turned to Junipa. "The business with your heart . . . that was never planned. Not I but the Light arranged that. I couldn't prevent it, for at that point I was also under the Light's influence. It was hard enough to resist it when I fetched Merle out of the Heart House." He shook his head sadly and looked at the floor. "It would have killed me for that if it were not dependent on me. It has made me into the master of Hell, and the Lilim respect and fear me. It would be difficult to find someone to take my place. And it would take a long time to build him up to what I am today." The shadow of a bitter smile flitted across his face. "But that has always been the fate of the Devil, hasn't it?

He can't simply quit like some captain of industry or abdicate like a king. He is what he is, forever."

Merle only looked at him while her thoughts whirled in circles, faster and faster. She caught herself trying to give her father a face, a younger version of Burbridge, without the wrinkles, without the gray in his hair and the weariness in his eyes.

"I must be grateful for the moments in which I can still be myself. But they are becoming ever fewer, and soon I will only be a puppet of the Light. Only then will I really deserve the name of Lord Light," he said cynically.

Was he actually expecting her to commiserate with him? Merle simply couldn't make him out. She looked into herself for hatred and contempt for everything that he'd done to her and Junipa and perhaps also to her father, but she wasn't able to find any shred of it.

"I wanted to see you, Merle," said Burbridge. "Even when you were still a little child. And I had so hoped the circumstances would be different. You should have met *me* first, not Lord Light. And now it has happened the other way around. I cannot expect that you will forgive me that."

Merle heard his words and understood their sense, but it didn't matter what he said: He remained a stranger to her. Just like her father.

"What happened to Steven?" she asked.

"He went through the mirror."

"Alone?"

Burbridge looked at the floor. "Yes."

"But without a guide out there he will become—"

"A phantom, I know. And I am not even sure if he didn't know that too. But I have never given up hope. If it is possible to look into other worlds, perhaps one could find him."

Junipa was staring at him with her mirror yes. "Was *that* what you wanted? For me to look for him?"

He lowered his eyes and said nothing more.

Merle nodded slowly. Suddenly she put all the pieces together. Junipa's mirror eyes, her lessons in the mirror workshop with Master Arcimboldo: Burbridge had determined her course since she'd left the orphanage.

"But why the messenger who offered to protect Venice from the Egyptians?"

"It was you I wanted to protect. And Arcimboldo, because I needed his mirrors."

"Then the business with the drop of blood from every Venetian wasn't anything but—"

This time it was Junipa who interrupted her. "He wanted to keep up appearances. And the picture people have of Hell. He's still Lord Light, after all. He has—" she said it very matter-of-factly—"duties."

"Is that true?" Merle asked him.

Burbridge sighed deeply, then nodded. "You can't understand that. This wrestling between me and the Light, the strength of its power . . . how it forces its thoughts on one and changes all that goes on in one. No one can comprehend that."

"Merle." The Flowing Queen ended her silence, speaking gently but urgently. *"We must get away from here. He is right when he speaks of how powerful the Stone Light is. And there are things that have to be done."*

Merle pondered briefly, then thought of something else. She turned to the professor again. "In the pyramid, when we were flying away from you . . . you said something there, you know a name. I didn't understand what you meant by that. Whose name?"

Burbridge came closer; he could have touched her with his hand now. But he didn't dare to. *"Her* name, Merle. The name of the Flowing Queen."

Is that true? she asked in her mind.

The Queen gave no answer.

"What would it change if I knew what she's named?"

"It isn't only her name," he said. "It has to do with who she really is."

Merle inspected him penetratingly. If it was some kind of a trick, she didn't understand what he was driving at. She tried to move the Queen to an explanation, but she seemed to be awaiting Burbridge's.

"Sekhmet," he said. "Her name is Sekhmet."

Merle dug into her memory. But there was nothing, no name that even resembled that one.

"Sekhmet?"

Burbridge smiled. "The ancient Egyptian goddess of the lions."

Is that so?

Hesitantly the Queen said, "*Yes.*"

But—

"In the old temple ruins and in the graves of the pharaohs she is depicted as a lioness. Ask her, Merle! Ask her if she was a lioness of stone."

"*More than that. I was a goddess, and yes, my body was that of a lioness. . . . At that time most of the gods still had their own bodies and wandered over the world like all other creatures. And who can say if we were really gods. We could not, in any case, but the idea pleased us and we began to give credence to the talk of the humans.*" She paused. "*Finally we also were convinced of our own omnipotence. That was the time when the humans began to hunt us. For the images of the gods are much easier to misuse for human purposes than the gods themselves. Images have no will and no desires. Statues stand for nothing but the goals of the rulers. So it has ever been. The word of a god is, in truth, only the word of the one who erected his statue.*"

Merle exchanged a look with Junipa. Her friend could not hear the Queen. In the mirror eyes Merle saw her own exhausted face and was afraid of herself.

How long ago was that? she asked the Queen in her mind.

"*Eons. Further back than the family tree of the Egyptians extends. Others worshipped me before, peoples whose names are long forgotten.*"

"Is she telling you the legend?" Burbridge asked. "If not, I will do it. Sekhmet, the mighty, wise, all-knowing Sekhmet, was impregnated by a moonbeam and then bore the first sphinx, the progenitor of the sphinx people."

The Son of the Mother! flashed into Merle's mind. Why didn't you tell me that?

"*Because then you would not have done what you have done. And what would it have changed? The dangers would have remained the same. But would you have faced them for an Egyptian goddess? I have never lied to you, Merle. I am the Flowing Queen. I am the one who protected Venice from the Egyptians. What I once was before—what role does that play?*"

A big one. Perhaps the biggest of all. Because you've brought me here. You know what the sphinxes are planning. Have probably always known it.

"*We are here to stop it. The Son of the Mother must not rise again. And if he does, I am the only one who can oppose him. For I am his mother and his lover. With him I bred the people of the sphinxes.*"

With your own *son*?

"*He was the son of the moonbeam. That is something different.*"

Oh, really?

Again Burbridge spoke. "Sekhmet can do nothing about it," he said, surprisingly defending the Queen, even if he could only guess what she was telling Merle. "What she thought was a moonbeam . . . was in truth something else. It was a beam of the Stone Light, when it plunged down to the Earth. Did it find its target intentionally? And why Sekhmet in particular? I don't know the answers to that. Probably the Light foresaw that its plunge deep into the interior of the Earth would bury it and that it would be hard to influence the creatures on the surface. Therefore—and this is only my theory as a scientist—I think that therefore the Light impregnated the lion goddess intentionally so that it could found its own race. A race of creatures that bore in them a piece of the Light, possibly without being aware of it. A people, in any case, that sometime could be taken over by the Light in order to carry out its orders on the surface. As the Lilim do in the interior of the Earth." Weary and worn out, he broke off. At the end his voice had sounded weaker and weaker, increasingly older and rougher.

You heard him, Merle said to the Queen.

"*Yes.*"

And?

The Queen seemed to hesitate, but then Merle heard the voice in her head again. "*It was I who killed the Son of the Mother. I felt too late that he bore the Light in him. It was too late because the people of the sphinxes were*

already born. I could only hinder him from rising to be
their ruler. But as it has turned out, I only achieved a post-
ponement. The sphinxes have become what I always
feared."

Then you went to the lagoon—

"In order to watch him. Just like Lalapeya and those
who came before her. Nevertheless, there was a great dif-
ference: The sphinxes worshipped him and kept watch to
keep anyone from desecrating his grave. I, on the other
hand, watched him to prevent his resurrection. Lalapeya
was the first one who guessed what he had in him. She had
no information, of course not, but she felt it. Especially
when she learned that the sphinxes were behind the
Egyptian Empire and saw the resurrection of the Son of the
Mother as the highest of their goals."

Merle understood. This was the connection she'd been
seeking, the connection between the sphinxes and the
Stone Light. The Pharaoh, the Horus priests, they'd all
been tools in the hands of the sphinxes.

The war, the destruction of the world, had that all not
been important, really? Had it always been only about
Venice and what was buried beneath it?

"With the prospect of world domination, the sphinxes
made the Horus priests and the Pharaoh compliant. But
their most important goal was always the lagoon. And I
was the only one who could keep them away from there."
Her voice faltered for a moment, as if she'd lost power

over it. Then she added more collectedly, *"I failed. But I have come into the stronghold of the sphinxes in order to set things right. With you, Merle."*

You wanted to go there from the beginning?

"No. In the beginning I thought that we would find help in Hell. I wanted to draw the Lilim into the war against the Empire. But I did not know how great the Stone Light's power over Burbridge already was. We have lost valuable time because of that. The Son of the Mother is already in the Iron Eye, I can sense him. Even Lalapeya cannot stop that. That is why she is there."

What will happen when he awakens?

"He will be for the Stone Light on the surface what Burbridge was here below—only incomparably more cruel and determined. He has more sphinx magic than anyone. There will be no doubt about him and very certainly no mirror room into which he withdraws from the influence of the Light. The Light will saturate the world as water does a sponge. And then it will stop for no one."

Merle's eyes sought Junipa, who had been watching her with curiosity and concern. If the Son of the Mother grasped power and brought the Empire under his control, Junipa would again fall under the control of the Stone Light. Like everyone else. Like Merle herself.

Burbridge and Junipa both knew what was going on in Merle's head. They couldn't hear the dialogue between her and the Queen, but they were observing Merle carefully, her features, each of her movements. Junipa was holding Merle's hand as tightly as before, as if she could somehow support her that way, help her to take in all the new information and process it.

The information and the Queen's admission had bowled her over, but she still summoned up the strength to concentrate on the most important things: on the Queen, on Junipa, and on the Son of the Mother.

And then there was Burbridge, who stood facing her, a heap of misery, an old man who looked as if he desperately needed a chair because he was hardly able to stand on his own.

"You must go," he said. "The Stone Light tolerates it sometimes when I withdraw here. But not often, and certainly not for as long as today."

Merle gently detached herself from Junipa, walked forward firmly, and for the first time held out her hand. He took it, and tears came to his eyes.

"What will it do?" she asked softly. "To you?"

"I am Lord Light. I will always be that. It will perhaps destroy these mirrors. But that is not bad. We have met, and I no longer need them. I have said to you what there is to say . . . or at least the most important things. There are other things that I feel and think and—" He broke off, shook his head, and began again. "I cannot withstand the Light much longer. It will strengthen its hold." Now the tears overflowed and rolled down his cheeks. "If we ever see each other again, I will finally have become him whom you met in Hell. The man who allowed Junipa's heart to be exchanged. Who rules the Lilim people like a despot. And who surrendered his free will to the Stone Light."

Merle's throat was tight. "You could come with us."

"I am too old," he said, shaking his head. "Without the power of the Light I would die."

Yet that's what you want, isn't it? Merle thought. But she didn't say it aloud. The thought hurt, even if she didn't want to admit it. She didn't want him to die. But she also didn't want him to be forever what humanity had long seen him as: the Devil, Satan in person.

He seemed to guess what she was thinking. "The Light has enveloped my soul. I'm too weak to go to my death of my own will. I've held out too long for that, fought too long. I could ask you, but that would be cruel and—"

"I can't do that!"

"I know." He smiled and looked strangely wise as he did so. "And perhaps that's best. Every world needs its devil, this one too. It needs the specter of evil in order to recognize why it's so important to defend the good. In certain ways I'm only fulfilling my duty. . . even the Stone Light does that. And someday people will again fear Hell as that which it's been all these millennia: a phantom, something that one may perhaps believe in but doesn't hold for real. Legends and myths and transfigured rumors, far, far from the daily life of human beings."

"But only if we succeed in stopping the sphinxes," said Junipa.

"That is the prerequisite." Burbridge pulled Merle to him and embraced her. She returned the gesture without thinking about it. "This story down here is not yours, my child. You are the heroine of the story up there. In Hell there are no heroes. Only those who are wrecked. It is not Lord Light who is your enemy. Your opponents are above: the sphinxes, the Son of the Mother. If you succeed in stopping them, it will be a long time before the Stone Light wins power on the upper surface again. If its loyal followers up there are destroyed, it is beaten in your part of the world. And as for this old man, it's best if you forget him again. For a few hundred or a few thousand years. The Light and I . . . Lord Light, I should say . . . we have enough to do in Hell. We need not concern ourselves with the upper world." He released her from his embrace, but his eyes continued to hold hers. "That is now your task alone."

"The Lilim won't attack the humans?"

"No. They have never done that. Not as an army, not to conquer their lands. There are individuals who've found their way up there, certainly . . . but they're only predators. There will be no war between above and below."

"But the Light will live on in Hell!"

"Powerful down here, but powerless on the surface.

Without its children, the sphinxes, it will probably need thousands of years before it dares a new attempt. Until then it is nothing but what the churches preach: the Tempter, the Evil One, the Fallen Angel, Lucifer—and for all of you, basically, as harmless as a ghost rattling its chains. If it is nothing more than a part of a religion, if it again becomes an empty expression, then it can no longer hurt anyone."

"*He is right,*" said the Flowing Queen excitedly. "*He really could be right.*"

"Go," said Burbridge once more, this time imploring. "Before—"

"Before it's too late?" Merle forced herself to smile. "I've read that somewhere."

Then Burbridge laughed and embraced her again. "You see, my child? Just a story. Nothing but a story."

He kissed her on the forehead, also kissed Junipa, then he stepped back.

The girls looked at him one last time, so they could remember the picture of Charles Burbridge, not Lord Light; the picture of an old man, not the Devil, which he would soon be again.

They departed the Hell of the Lilim through the mirror and walked back into their own world.

7

THE ABDUCTION

"THEY'RE GONE," JUNIPA SAID.

"What?"

"They're not in the hiding place anymore." Piercing the silver veil of the mirror world, Junipa was looking into the Iron Eye, into the room where they'd left the comrades. "There's no one there now," she said in distress.

"Where did they go?"

"I don't know. I have to look for them."

Merle swore because she couldn't see through the mirror herself. All she saw were blurry forms and colors, but no clear pictures. At the moment she couldn't even make out which mirror the hiding place had lain behind.

"There's . . . there's been a fight," Junipa said. "The sphinxes—they discovered them."

"Oh, no!"

"There are three men lying on the floor . . . three spies. They're dead. The others are gone."

"And Vermithrax?"

"I don't see him."

"But you can't miss him!"

Junipa turned toward her, and for perhaps the first time since Merle had known her, her voice sounded irritated.

"Be patient, will you? I have to concentrate."

Merle bit her lower lip and kept quiet. Her knees were trembling.

Junipa let go of her hand and looked around, turning in all directions among the mirrors. "The Iron Eye is so big. There are too many mirrors. They could be any-where."

"Then take me back into the hiding place."

"Are you really sure? That could be dangerous."

"I want to see it with my own eyes. Otherwise it's so . . . so unreal."

Junipa nodded. "Stay close by me. Just in case we have to disappear again fast." She took Merle by the hand again and whispered the glass word, and they walked through a mirror as if through a curtain of moonlight.

The door of the room was shattered into hundreds of mirror fragments, which covered the floor like strewn razor blades. The wall mirrors also showed cracks in several places. One wall, to the girls' right, was completely destroyed, and it took only seconds for them to realize that this was the way Vermithrax had fled from the sphinxes. The stone wall beneath the remaining glass looked like an open mouth full of missing teeth.

"There must have been many of them," Junipa declared thoughtfully. "Otherwise he wouldn't have run away. He's much stronger than they are."

Merle had gone down in a crouch beside the three dead men. She quickly saw that the Czarists were beyond help. Andrej was not among them. Merle remembered a fifth spy, a red-haired hulk of a man, who'd looked particularly grotesque in his mummy clothing. He was also missing.

"Merle!"

She looked up, first at Junipa, who'd uttered the terrified cry, then toward the door.

A sphinx was rushing toward them, his speed hypnotic. The sight froze her. But Junipa was already beside her, grabbed her, spoke the word, and pulled her through the nearest mirror. Behind them sounded a shout of surprised fury and then they heard a shrill grinding as the massive sphinx soldier crashed against the glass. A crack appeared inside the mirror world for a moment, then it was extinguished, like a pencil stroke that someone erased from the top to the bottom.

Merle was out of breath. The knowledge of how closely they'd escaped death gradually spread through her. Her heart hammered in her chest, hard and jabbing.

Junipa's eyes remained expressionless, but her face showed how angry she was. "I told you to stay by me! That was pretty close!"

"I thought perhaps I could still help someone."

Junipa looked as if she were going to make an angry reply, but then her expression resolved into its usual gentleness. "Yes. Of course." She looked encouragingly at Merle. "I'm sorry."

They smiled shyly at each other, then Junipa took Merle by the hand. Together they walked on.

Soon Merle again had the feeling of being lost and had to rely on Junipa's sense of direction. Now and again they stopped. Junipa looked around, almost sensing, like a predator prowling for prey, touched a mirror wall once or twice, and then hurried on.

"Here!" she said finally, pointing to a mirror. It seemed to Merle that it shone a little more brightly than the others, in an orangey, fiery light.

"There he is! That's Vermithrax!"

"Wait. Let me look first." Junipa stepped forward until the tip of her nose touched the glass. When she whispered the word, the surface clouded before her lips. She shoved her face through just far enough to see to the other side, dove through her white breath on the glass as if it were a pitcher of fresh milk. Merle held her hand and had the feeling that Junipa's fingers grew colder the longer she stayed part in the mirror world, part in the Iron Eye.

She whispered her friend's name.

A wavelike shuddering ran through the mirror when Junipa pulled her face back. "They're there. All four."

"Seth too?"

"Yes. He's fighting beside Andrej."

"Really?" The idea surprised her.

Junipa nodded. "What do we do now?"

We have to go to them, Merle told herself. Have to help them. Have to stop the sphinxes from completing their plan. But how? She might be the granddaughter of the Devil, the daughter of a sphinx—but she was still only a fourteen-year-old girl. Any sphinx could kill her with a single stroke. And she didn't want Junipa to be stabbed.

"I know what you're thinking," said Junipa.

Merle stared past her at the mirror and the light behind it, at the twitching forms, too distorted for her to recognize figures in them. She knew that Vermithrax and the others were fighting for their lives over there, and yet no sound of it crossed over the threshold of the mirror world. No clattering of weapons, no cries, no panting or grim moans. The world could have been destroyed on the other side, but here behind the mirrors it would have been nothing more than pretty fireworks of color and silver.

"Something's different from before," Junipa said.

"What?"

Junipa crouched, put one hand on the glass at floor level, whispered the word, and reached through. When she pulled her fingers back, they were clenched into a fist. She held it before Merle's face and opened it.

Merle stared at what she saw in front of her. Then stretched out a finger and touched it.

"Ice," she whispered breathlessly.

"Snow," said Junipa. "It's only hard because I pressed it together."

"But that means that Winter is here! Here in the Iron Eye!"

"He can make it snow even inside buildings?" Junipa frowned. Merle had told her of Winter and his search for his beloved Summer. But she still had trouble imagining a season as a flesh-and-blood being who roamed through the mirrored passages of the Eye.

Merle made her decision. "I want to go over there."

Junipa threw the snow to the floor, where it dissolved into water as soon as it landed. She sighed softly, but finally she nodded. "Yes, we really have to do something." She thought for a moment and added, "But don't go all the way through the mirror. As long as you have an arm or a foot on the other side, the mirror will remain permeable. In an emergency, we only need to jump back."

Merle agreed, even if she hardly heard what Junipa said. She was much too stirred up, her head whirling.

Hand in hand they walked through the mirror.

Blinding brightness greeted them. A snowfield that was lengthened into infinity by the walls and the ceiling. A wave of noise and fury slammed against them, worse than anything Merle had expected. Vermithrax let out a shattering roar, while he took on two sphinxes at the same time. Andrej and Seth were fighting back-to-back. The red-haired spy lay lifeless on the floor; the blow of a sickle sword had felled him. There were several mummy soldiers in the hall. Beside them Merle counted three sphinxes. Another lay motionless in the entrance.

"Merle!" Vermithrax had seen her; he blocked the blow of a sword with his bare paw and with the other pulled his claws down the chest of the sphinx. Blood flowed into the snow and was soon covered by the body of the collapsed sphinx. The second sphinx hesitated before he resolved on a renewed attack. When he saw that his sword blow bounced off the lion's glowing obsidian body as if it were a wall, he retreated. Vermithrax made a few lunges after him but then let his opponent run.

Andrej and Seth were fighting together against the third sphinx and the three mummy soldiers. The undead were no great help to their leader, continually standing in the way or stumbling into the attack of the sphinx. Finally he also let out an angry cry and stormed away, straight across the hall and through the high door, behind which still more snow stretched.

Junipa was still standing in front of the mirror wall, half in this world, half in the mirror world. Merle had taken her advice to heart and until now had endeavored not to lose contact with the mirror. But when she saw that the sphinxes were fleeing, she was about to let go of Junipa's hand and run over to Vermithrax.

Suddenly someone seized her, tore her away from Junipa, and flung her to one side. With a scream she crashed against one of the mirrors and fell to her knees. At once her dress was sucking up ice-cold wetness.

When Merle looked up, she saw Seth. He'd grasped Junipa's hand, pushed off, and pulled her with him through the mirror wall. No glass splintered, and Merle knew the reason for it: The glass door was open as long as Junipa had not left the mirror. The glass word remained in effect for her and anyone she touched. For Seth, too.

"No!" Merle leaped up and ran through the snow to the mirror. But she already knew that she was too late.

Seth and Junipa were gone. Merle wanted to follow them, against her better judgment, and she struck the glass with her shoulder. The glass wall creaked, but it held.

"No!" She shouted again, kicked her foot against the glass, and hammered on it with her fists. With watery eyes she stared into the mirror, but instead of her friend and the high priest, she saw only herself, with wild, straggling hair, red eyes, and shining cheeks. Her dress was wet with snow, but she hardly felt the cold.

"Merle," said Vermithrax quietly, suddenly beside her.

She didn't hear him, drummed against the mirror again, whirled around, and sank down with her back against the glass. In despair she rubbed her eyes, but the brightness around her now blinded her even more. Light reflections formed glistening stars and circles, all clear figures blurred.

One of them was Vermithrax. Another was Andrej, whom the stone lion had dragged with him and laid down between them in the snow. Somewhere in the background lay the mummy soldiers in the midst of gray fountains of dust.

"She's gone," said the lion.

"I see that, damn it!"

"Andrej is dying, Merle."

"I—" She broke off, stared at Vermithrax, then the Czarist, who stretched out a hand to her from the ground. He whispered something in his mother tongue, and it was obvious that he saw in Merle someone other than herself.

Vermithrax nodded to her. "Take his hand," he whispered.

Merle sank to her knees and embraced Andrej's cold fingers with both hands. Her thoughts were still with

Junipa, whom she'd now lost for the second time, but she did her best to concentrate on the dying man. *Unreal* kept thundering through her mind over and over. Everything is so unreal.

Andrej's free hand grasped her shoulder, so hard that it hurt, and pulled her forward. The fingers climbed to her neck. Just as Merle was about to pull back, he was able to take hold of the leather band on which she wore the chicken's foot. The sign of the Baba Yaga. The sign of his goddess.

Merle would have liked to wipe the tears from her eyes, but she knew she mustn't let go of him now. No matter what happened around her: Andrej deserved to die in peace. He was a brave man, as were his companions; they'd taken the risk of giving up their camouflage for the girls and the lion. They could have been finished off by that first sphinx alone, but Andrej had struck him for them. Perhaps because after all the months in the Iron Eye he'd been glad to meet a living, breathing human again.

Andrej clung with one hand to the chicken's foot on her neck while he murmured words in Russian, perhaps a prayer, perhaps something else. Several times there was a word that Merle thought was the name of a woman or a girl. "His daughter" flashed through her mind. He'd told her, very briefly, after he'd led all three of them into the hiding place, about his daughter, whom he'd left many thousands of miles away.

Then Andrej died. With trembling hands she had to loosen his fingers from the pendant.

Vermithrax snorted softly.

"We have to get away from here!" he said finally, and it seemed to Merle that these seven words described their journey best. Away from Venice, away from Axis Mundi, an everlasting flight. And her destination seemed always to slide into the distance again.

Vermithrax spoke again. "The sphinxes will send out the alarm."

Merle nodded absently. She crossed Andrej's hands on his chest, without knowing if this gesture was understood in his homeland. She lightly stroked his cheek with the back of her hand before she stood up.

Vermithrax looked at her out of his huge lion eyes. "You are very brave. Much braver than I thought."

She gave a sob and began to cry, but this time she quickly got herself under control. "What about Junipa?"

"We can't follow her."

"I *know* that. But still we must do something—"

"*We must get out of here! Fast.*" At moments like this, Merle sometimes forgot that she wasn't alone in her thoughts. When the Queen abruptly cut into the conversation, she started, as if suddenly there were someone standing behind her and bellowing in her ear. "*Vermithrax is right. We have to keep them from calling the Son of the Mother back to life.*"

"The Son of the Mother can go jump in a lake!" Merle shouted angrily, so that Vermithrax heard it too. He raised an eyebrow in amazement. "Seth has abducted Junipa, and at the moment that's more important to me than some kind of sphinx god and its mother!"

That was clear, she hoped. But the Queen wouldn't be moved. If there was anything on which she was an expert, it was persistence. Nerve-deadening, pitiless persistence. *"Your world will be destroyed, Merle. It will be destroyed, if you and I do not do something to prevent it."*

"My world is already destroyed," she said sadly. "From the moment you and I met each other." She didn't mean it sarcastically, and there was no malice in her voice. Every word was sincere, honestly felt: Her world—a new, unexpected one, but *her own*—had been Arcimboldo's workshop, with all its pros and cons, with Dario and the other rowdies, but also with Junipa and Eft and a place where she felt she belonged. The appearance of the Queen had brought an end to it all.

The Queen was silenced for a moment, but then she broke into the gloomy silence in Merle's head. *"Do not blame me. After the attack of the Egyptians, nothing was the way it had been."*

Merle knew very well that she was putting blame in the wrong place. "I'm sorry," she said, and yet she didn't really mean it. She couldn't help it, not here, not today, not beside Andrej's body and in front of the mirror into which Junipa had vanished as if down a silvery throat. She could say she was sorry, but she couldn't really feel it.

"Merle," said Vermithrax urgently, "please! We have to go!"

She swung onto his back. She cast a last sorrowful look at the mirror through which Junipa and Seth had disappeared, and then it was only one among many again, a facet on the many cut surfaces of a precious jewel.

"Where are we, anyway?" she asked as Vermithrax bore her through the door of the hall, stopped in the passage outside for a moment, then turned to the right. The snow inside the building lay high, twelve to sixteen inches, and it was churned up by the paws of the sphinxes and the boots of the mummy soldiers.

"Quite a way down below the spies' room." The obsidian lion gazed ahead tensely as he spoke. "We ran down stairs almost the whole time. Andrej knew the way very well. And probably his friends did too. But I couldn't understand what they were saying."

"*Andrej knew it,*" said the Queen. "*He knew that the Son of the Mother is here in the stronghold.*"

Merle passed the information along to Vermithrax. He agreed: "Seth told us while you were gone."

"Why did he do that?"

"Maybe to keep us busy while he was thinking about how to get at Junipa."

Merle deflated a little further.

"Seth only had revenge in his head," the lion added.

"Why not?" said the Queen. *"If that helps us to stop the Son of the Mother."*

Merle would have loved to take her by the shoulders and shake her, but the shoulders of the Queen were now her own, and that would have looked really silly. "Good," she said after a while, "then just tell us what we should do if we suddenly stumble on him by accident."

"May I?" asked the Queen, with unwonted politeness.

"Help yourself."

Immediately the Queen took over Merle's voice and told Vermithrax very briefly who and what the Son of the Mother was. And what role she herself played in this affair.

"You are the mother of the sphinxes?" asked Vermithrax in astonishment. "The great Sekhmet?"

"Only Sekhmet. That is enough."

"The lion goddess!"

"Now he is starting that business too," said the Queen in Merle's thoughts, and this time Merle could not suppress a faint grin.

"Is that really true?" asked Vermithrax.

"No, I am only inventing it to keep us from getting bored in this accursed fortress," the Queen said through Merle's mouth.

"Forgive me."

"No reason to become unctuous."

"Sekhmet is the goddess of all lions," said Vermithrax. "Also of my people."

"*More than that,*" whispered the Queen to Merle, before she said aloud, "If you like. But I have not been a goddess for a long time—if I ever was one."

Vermithrax sounded baffled. "I don't understand."

"Just act the way you did before. No 'Great Sekhmet' here or 'goddess' there. Agreed?"

"Certainly," he said humbly.

"Don't worry about it," said Merle, when her own voice belonged to her again. "You get used to her."

"*A little humility would probably not hurt,*" said the Queen peevishly.

Vermithrax carried them down more steps, deeper and deeper, and at each landing the snow became higher, the cold more cutting.

Merle looked into the mirrors, which lengthened the white into infinity, and made a decision. "We have to find Winter."

"*We have to—,*" the Queen began, but Merle interrupted her.

"Alone we have no chance anyway. But together with Winter . . . who knows."

"*He will not help us. His mind is only on his search for Summer.*"

"Perhaps one thing has something to do with the other?" Merle twisted one side of her mouth in a cool smile.

"But the fastest way—"

"At the moment I'm for the safest way. What do you think, Vermithrax?"

"Everything the goddess commands."

"A lion with principles."

Merle rolled her eyes. "I don't care. We're looking for Winter! Vermithrax, keep walking to where the snow is highest."

"You will freeze to death."

"Then we'll both freeze."

"I will try to prevent that."

"Very kind."

In the middle of a stairwell, the fourth or fifth since their leaving the hall, Vermithrax stopped so abruptly that Merle slid into his mane face-first; it felt as if she'd dived into a forest of glistening underwater plants.

"What is it?"

He growled and looked around warily. "Something's wrong here."

"Are we being followed?"

"No."

"Observed?"

"That's just it. Since the fight we haven't seen any more sphinxes and mummies."

"That's all right with me."

"Come on, Merle, don't pretend to be stupid. You know what I mean."

Of course she knew. But she'd been trying the whole time to suppress it and would have liked to be able to do it a while longer. Besides, she was in the mood to quarrel. With the Queen, even with Vermithrax. She didn't rightly understand where all this anger at everyone and everything came from. Really it was Seth who'd betrayed them and abducted Junipa. Wrong! Abducted Junipa, yes—but betrayed? He'd done nothing to surrender Merle and the others to the sphinxes. He was always pursuing his own personal ends and, looking at it objectively, he had simply seized an advantage. Junipa was supposed to take him somewhere, that much was certain. For she was the key to a fast, effortless change of location. But where? To Heliopolis? Or some other place here in the Eye?

"It's as if this whole damned fortress were dead all of a sudden!" Vermithrax also sounded irritated. His huge nose sniffed the air in the circle of the stairwell, while his eyes swept alertly around. "There must still be someone somewhere."

"Perhaps they have something to do somewhere else." For instance, with Winter, Merle added in her mind.

"Or with the Son of the Mother," said the Queen.

Merle imagined the scene: a huge hall in which hundreds of sphinxes were gathered. All were staring raptly at the body on its bier. Singing hung in the air, soft murmuring. The words of a priest or a leader. Grotesque apparatus and machines were turned on. Electrical charges sparked between metal balls and steel coils with many turns of wire. Fluids bubbled in glass beakers, hot steam shot out of vents to the ceiling. All was reflected dozens of times in the towering silver walls.

Then a cry, leaping like flame from one sphinx to the next. Strident masks of triumph, open mouths, wide eyes, roars of laughter, of joy, of relief, but also of barely concealed anxiety. Priests and scientists, who swarmed around the Son of the Mother like flies around a piece of carrion. A dark eyelid that slowly opened. Under it a black eyeball, dried and wrinkled like a prune. And in it, caught like a curse in a dusty tomb, an increasingly bright spark of devilish intelligence.

"Merle?"

Vermithrax's voice.

"Merle?" More urgent now. "Did you hear that?"

She came alert. "Huh?"

"Did you hear that?"

"What?"

"Listen carefully."

Merle tried to comprehend what Vermithrax meant. It was only with difficulty that she was able to free herself from the picture that her mind had conjured up: the ancient, dark eye and in it the awakening understanding of the Son of the Mother.

Now she heard it.

A howling.

Again the image of a monstrous gathering of all the sphinxes arose in her. The murmuring, the singing, the sound of the rituals.

But the howling had another source.

"Sounds like a storm," Merle said.

She'd hardly spoken when something rushed at them out of the depths of the stairwell. Vermithrax bent way over the railing; Merle had to cling tightly to his mane in order not to slide down over his head into the well.

A white wall rose up out of the mirrored chasm.

Fog, she thought at first.

Snow!

A snowstorm that seemed to come directly from the heart of the Arctic, a fist of ice and cold and unimaginable force.

Vermithrax raised his wings and folded them together over Merle like two giant hands, which pressed her firmly to his back. The howling grew deafening and finally so loud that she could scarcely perceive it as sound, a blade that cut through her auditory canal and carved up her understanding. She had the feeling that her living body was turning to ice, just like the dead gull she'd found on the roof of the orphanage one winter. The bird had looked as if it had simply fallen from heaven, the wings still spread, the eyes open. When Merle had lost her balance for a moment on the smooth roof slope, it had slipped out of her hand and a wing broke off as if it were made of porcelain.

The storm passed them like a swarm of howling ghosts. When it was over and the wind in the stairwell died down, the layer of snow on the steps had almost doubled.

"Was *that* Winter?" Vermithrax asked numbly. Ice crystals glittered on his coat, a strange contrast to his body glow, which gave off no heat and was not able to melt the ice.

Merle sat up on his back, ran both hands through her hair, and wiped the wet strands out of her face. The tiny little hairs in her nose were frozen, and for a while it was easier to breathe through her mouth.

"I don't know," she got out with a groan. "But if Winter had been in that storm somewhere, he'd certainly have seen us. He wouldn't just have run past us. Or flown. Or whatever." Dazedly she knocked the snow from her dress. It was completely frozen through, and at her knees the material was almost stiff. "It's time we found Summer."

"*We?*" said the Queen in alarm.

Merle nodded. "Without her we're going to freeze. And then it doesn't matter anymore if your son wakes up or not."

"The sphinxes," Vermithrax said. "They're frozen, aren't they? That's why there aren't any down here anymore. The cold has killed them."

Merle didn't think it was that simple. But sometimes Fate played tricks on one. And why couldn't it affect the other side once in a while, for a change?

The obsidian lion began moving again. He was trudging through high snow, but he found the steps without any trouble and walked on with amazing sure-footedness. Even a little dampness could turn the mirrored floors of the Iron Eye into slides; for the moment they almost had to be grateful for the snow, for it padded the lion's steps and kept his paws from sliding on the icy glass floor.

"In any case, the storm came from Winter," Merle said after a while. "Although I don't believe he was anywhere inside it. But this must be the right path." After pondering a little she added, "Vermithrax, did Andrej say where the Son of the Mother would be brought?"

"If he did, he said it in Russian."

And you? Merle turned to the Queen. Do you know where he is?

"*No.*"

Perhaps where Summer is also?

"*How do you fig—*" The Queen broke off and said instead, "*You really think there is more hidden in Summer's disappearance, do you?*"

Burbridge told Winter something, Merle thought. Therefore Winter is looking for her here in the Iron Eye. And if Summer had something to do with the power of the Empire?

"*You are thinking of the sunbarks?*"

Yes. But also about the mummies. And all those things that can only be explained by magic. Why didn't the priests awaken the Pharaoh a hundred years ago? Or five hundred years ago? Perhaps because they only got the strength to from Summer! They call it magic, but maybe it's something else. Machines that we don't know, that are driven with a strength that they somehow . . . I don't know, *steal* from Summer. You said it yourself: Seth is not a powerful magician. He may command a few illusions, but real magic? He's a scientist, just like all the other Horus priests. And like Burbridge. The only ones who actually understand something about magic are the sphinxes.

The Queen thought that over. *"Summer as a kind of living furnace?"*

Like the steam furnaces in the factories outside on the lagoon islands, thought Merle.

"That sounds quite mad."

Just like goddesses who bring a whole people into the world with a moonbeam.

This time she felt the Queen laugh. Softly and suppressed, but she laughed. After a while she said, *"The suboceanic kingdoms possessed such machines. No one knew exactly how they were driven. They used them in their war against the Lords of the Deep, against the ancestors of the Lilim."*

Merle could see how all the mosaic pieces were gradually fitting together into a whole. Possibly the Horus priests had stumbled on remains or drawings from the suboceanic cultures. Perhaps with their help they'd succeeded in awakening the Pharaoh or building their sunbarks. Suddenly it filled her with bitter satisfaction that the cities of the suboceanic kingdoms had fallen in ruins on the ocean floor eons ago. The prospect of the same thing happening to the Empire suddenly moved quite a bit closer.

"There's someone coming!" Vermithrax stopped.

Merle was startled. "From down below?"

The lion mane whipped back and forth in a nod. "I can sense them."

"Sphinxes?"

"At least one."

"Can you get any closer to the railing? Maybe we can see them then."

"Or they us," replied the lion, shaking his head. "There's only one possibility: We fly past them." Until now he'd avoided flying down, because the shaft in the center of the spiral staircase was very narrow, and he was afraid of breaking his wings on the sharp edges. And a wounded Vermithrax was the last thing they could bear.

However, the way things looked now, they had to try it.

They wasted no time. Merle clung to him. Vermithrax rose up and leaped over the railing and down into the chasm. They had dared such a steep flight once before, during the escape from the Campanile in Venice. But this one was worse. The cold bit into Merle's face and through her clothing, she couldn't brush away the snow particles that got into her eyes, and her heart was galloping as if it were trying to outrace her. She could hardly breathe.

They passed two windings of the stairs, then three, four, five. At the height of the sixth, Vermithrax braked his nosedive with such force that Merle thought at first they'd hit something—stone, steel, perhaps an invisible mirror floor in the stairwell. But then the lion leveled and floated with gentle wing beats in the center of the stairwell, with emptiness over and under them and in front of them—

"But that can't be—" Then Merle's voice failed her and she wasn't even certain whether she'd actually said the words aloud or only thought them.

It could almost have been their own reflection: a figure who was riding on the back of a half-human creature, which was climbing the steps on four legs. A boy, only a little older than Merle, with tousled hair and cozy fur clothing. The creature on which he sat was a female sphinx. Her arms were scantily bandaged all the way to the elbows. The four paws of her lion lower body seemed to be unharmed; she had borne her rider securely up the steps.

The sphinx was beautiful, much more beautiful than Merle had imagined her, and not even her weary, emaciated look could alter that. She had black hair falling smoothly over her shoulders down to the place where human and lion melted together.

The boy opened his eyes wide, his lips moved, but his words were lost in the rushing of the lion wings and the raging of distant snowstorms below.

Merle whispered his name.

And Vermithrax attacked.

8

AMENOPHIS

SETH HAD LONG CEASED TO THREATEN HER WITH HIS DRAWN sword. It was unnecessary, as they both knew. And it lacked a certain dignity for a man like him to be pointing his sickle blade at a girl like Junipa, half as big and very much weaker.

Junipa was sure that he wouldn't do anything to her as long as she obeyed him. Basically, she thought, she was of no importance to him, just like Merle and the others, just like the whole world. Seth had built up the Empire with sweat and blood and privation, and now he would demolish it again with his own hands, or at least swing the hammer to strike the first blow.

"To Venice," he'd said, after he pushed her back into the mirror world. "Inside the palace." As if Junipa were a gondolier on the Grand Canal.

When she'd looked at him for a long moment in disbelief, a spark of doubt had appeared in his eyes. As if he weren't really aware of her capabilities.

But then she said "Yes," and nothing else. And started on the way.

He was now walking some distance behind her, almost soundlessly. Only now and then the sword in his belt struck its point against a mirror edge, and the screeching that it caused rushed like a call of alarm through the glass labyrinth of the mirror world. But there was no one there who could have heard it; or if there was, no one showed himself, not even the phantoms.

Junipa didn't ask Seth what he had in mind. For one thing, she already guessed. For another, he wouldn't have given her an answer anyway.

Before, when she'd walked into the Iron Eye with Merle, she had felt again the grip of the Stone Light. A devilish pain flamed up in her chest, just as if someone were trying to bend her ribs apart from the inside like the bars on a cage. The fragment of the Stone Light that had been inserted into her in Hell reminded her emphatically that sooner or later it would again gain power over her, when she left the mirror world or just gradually when she began to feel secure. The stone in her chest was threat and dark promise equally.

Behind the mirrors she felt better, the pain was gone, the pressure vanished. Her stone heart did not beat, but somehow it kept her alive, the Devil might know why — and indeed, *he* certainly did know.

Considering her situation, the threat of the Horus priest seemed far less dreadful to her. She could run away from Seth, or at least attempt it — but there was no outrunning the Light. At least not in her world. The Light might lose interest in her for a while, the way it did after her flight from Hell, but it was always there. Always ready to seize her, to influence her, and to set her on her friends.

No, it was good that she wasn't in the Iron Eye with Merle. She was beginning to feel sure in the mirror world. Everything in this labyrinth of silver glass was somehow familiar. Her eyes led her, let her see what no one else saw, and that made her aware how very much Seth had put himself into her hands. Perhaps he wasn't even aware of it himself.

To Venice, she thought. Yes, she would take him to Venice if he wanted it.

Just as in Hell, in the mirror world there was no difference between day and night. However, now and then the darkness appeared to descend on the other side of one of the mirrors or the morning to dawn; then the shine of the silver changed, the flickering of the colors. Their light also fell on Junipa and Seth and bathed them sometimes in one color, sometimes in another, from dark turquoise to milky lemon yellow. Once Junipa turned to the priest and saw the flaming red from a mirror gush over his face and strengthen his determined, warriorlike expression. Then again a gentle, heavenly blue covered him, and the hardness left his features.

In this place between places there were still many wonders to explore. The riddle of the colors and their effect was only one of countless mysteries.

She wasn't able to say how much time passed before they reached their destination. They didn't speak about it: It was several hours, certainly. But while behind one mirror only moments passed, behind the next it might perhaps be years. Still a secret, still a challenge.

Seth stopped beside her and regarded the mirror that rose in front of him. "Is that it?"

She wondered if the priest were filled with rage alone or whether there wasn't also a little fear, a trace of insecurity in the light of the grandeur of the environment. But Seth betrayed nothing of what was going on inside him. He hid his true nature behind anger and bitterness, and his only drive was the desire for revenge.

"Yes," she said, "behind it lies Venice. The chamber of the Pharaoh in the Doge's palace."

He touched the mirror surface with the palm of his hand, as if he hoped to be able to pass through it without Junipa and the glass word. He bent forward, breathed on it, and rubbed the cloud away with his fist, as if he were removing a spot of dirt. If there had been a spot there, it would only have been the hate in him, something that would not be simply wiped away.

Seth regarded his mirror image for a little while longer, as though he couldn't believe that the man in the glass was a reflection of himself. Then he blinked, took a deep breath, and drew his sickle sword.

"Are you ready?" Junipa asked, and she already saw the answer in him. He nodded.

"I'll take a look into the room first," she said. "You'll want to know if the Pharaoh is alone."

To her astonishment, he refused. "Not necessary."

"But—"

"You understood me, didn't you?"

"There could be ten sphinxes there standing around the Pharaoh! Or a hundred!"

"Perhaps. But I don't think so. I think they're gone. The sphinxes are on the way back into the Iron Eye or are already gathered there. They've got what they wanted. Venice doesn't interest them anymore." He laughed coldly. "And Amenophis not at all."

"The sphinxes have abandoned him?"

"Just as he did the Horus priests."

Junipa said nothing. The Pharaoh's betrayal had struck Seth more deeply than he would have thought possible. The two agreed on nothing, and yet Amenophis was anchored in his soul. Not as a human being, for Seth was indifferent to him, yes, he even despised him. But as his creation, which he'd awakened to life and which stood for all that Seth had once believed in.

What Seth was planning was far more than only the taking of another's life. It was a betrayal of himself, of his goals, of all the possibilities that his pact with Amenophis had opened to him. It was also a clean break with his own works in all the decades since he planned and supervised the reawakening of the Pharaoh.

Either way, it was the end.

Junipa took hold of his arm, whispered the glass word, and pulled him through the mirror.

At once the pressure was there in her chest again, the seeking and squeezing and dragging of the Light.

The huge room behind the mirror was empty. At least at first sight. But then she discovered the divan of jaguar skins, which emerged from the semidarkness on the other side of the room. It was night in Venice, and also here in the salon; only a weak glow came through the window. Torchlight from the Piazza San Marco, she guessed. It rested softly on the patterns of the carved panels, on the brushstrokes of the oil paintings and frescoes, on the crystal pendants of the chandeliers.

Something moved on the divan. A dark silhouette in front of a still darker hill of skins.

No one spoke.

Junipa felt as if she weren't really there, as if she were

observing the scene from a faraway place. As in a dream. *Yes,* she thought, *a great, horrible dream, and I can do nothing except watch. Not take part, not run away, only look on.*

Glass shattered behind her and tinkled onto the floor in a cascade of silver droplets. Seth had smashed the wall mirror through which they'd entered the salon. No possibility of retreat anymore. Junipa looked around hastily, but there were no other mirrors here, and she doubted she would get far enough in the corridors of the palace to find another.

Amenophis rose from his divan of jaguar skins, a small, slender figure, who moved slightly bent, as if he carried a terrible weight on his shoulders.

"Seth," he said wearily. Junipa wondered if he were drunk. His voice sounded numb and at the same time very young.

Amenophis, the resurrected Pharaoh and leader of the Empire, stepped into the half light from the window.

He was still a child. Only a boy, who had been turned into something that he might never have become without gold paint and makeup. He was no older than twelve or thirteen, at least a year younger than herself. And yet he'd commanded his armies to rule the world for four decades.

Junipa stood stock-still among the ruins of the mirror. The shards were spread wide over the dark parquet. It looked as though she were swimming in the middle of a starry sky.

Seth walked past her up to the Pharaoh. If he was looking around for guards or other opponents, he didn't betray
it by any motion. He stared straight ahead at the ordinary-
looking boy who waited for him in front of the divan.

"Are they all gone?" he asked.

Amenophis did not move. Said nothing.

"They've left you, haven't they." Seth's tone was
without any arrogance or spiteful pleasure. A statement,
nothing else. "The sphinxes are gone. And without the
Horus priests . . . yes, what are you without us,
Amenophis?"

"We are the Pharaoh," said the boy. He was smaller than
Junipa, very slight and unprepossessing. He sounded sulky
but also a little resigned, as if in his heart he'd accepted his
fate. And then Junipa realized there would be no spectacular
final battle between the two of them. No wild swordplay, no
murderous duel over tables and chairs, no antagonists who
swung through the room from the lamps and the curtains.

This was the end, and it was coming quietly and without tumult. Like the end of a serious disease, a gentle
death after a long illness.

"Were all the priests executed?" asked Seth.

"You know that."

"You could have let them go."

"We had given our word: If you failed, they would die."

"You already broke your word once when you
betrayed the Horus priests."

"No reason to do it a second time." The boy's smile belied his words as he added, "Even we learn from our mistakes sometimes."

"Not today."

Amenophis took a few steps to the right, to a large water basin beside the divan. He put his hands in and washed them absently. Junipa almost expected that he would pull out a weapon and point it at Seth. But Amenophis only rubbed his fingers clean and shook them briefly, so that the droplets whirled in all directions, before he again turned to the priest.

"Our armies are inconceivably large. Millions upon millions. We have the strongest men as guards, fighters from Nubia and the old Samarkand. But we are tired. So tired."

"Why don't you call for your guards?"

"They left when the sphinxes disappeared. The priests were dead, and suddenly there were only living corpses in this palace." He let out a cackling laugh, which didn't sound either real or especially full of humor. "The Nubians looked at the mummies, then us, and they realized that they were the only ones alive in this building."

He had the council murdered, flashed through Junipa's mind. *The entire City Council of Venice.*

"They left us a short time later; secretly, of course. Though we had long observed what was going on in their heads." He shrugged. "The Empire is destroying itself."

"No," said Seth. "You destroyed it. At the moment when you had my priests executed."

"You never loved us."

"But we respected you. We Horus priests were always loyal and would have continued to be, if you had not given the sphinxes preference over us."

"The sphinxes were only interested in their own intrigues, that is true."

"Insight too late."

For the first time Amenophis spoke of himself in the singular. "What shall I say?" The most powerful boy in the world smiled, but it distorted his face like his reflection on the moving surface of the water basin. "I have slept for four thousand years, and I can do it again. But the world will not forget me, will it? That is also a form of immortality. No one can forget what I have done to the world."

"And are you proud of that?" asked Junipa, her first words since her arrival. Amenophis didn't deign to answer her, not even with a glance. But suddenly something became clear to her: The two were speaking Egyptian with each other; and yet she understood what they said. And at the same time she understood what Arcimboldo had meant when he told her, "As guide through the mirror world, you are a master of all voices, all tongues. For what good would a guide be if he didn't know the language of the lands through which he led others?" How could she have guessed before what that was going to mean? It was still hard for her to grasp the whole truth now. Did that really mean that she understood each of the languages that were spoken in the countless worlds? *All voices, all tongues* echoed through her mind, and she grew quite dizzy with it.

Amenophis pulled her out of her astonishment. "Immortality is better than what you gave me," he said to Seth. "A few decades, no more. Perhaps they would have made a century. But you were already tired of me, weren't you? How long would you have tolerated me? You wanted to take my place . . . poor Seth, you were quite ill with envy and ambition. And who can blame you for that? You were the one who solved the riddles of the suboceanic kingdoms. You gave the Empire all its power. And now look at you! Only a man without hair and with a sword in his hand that he never even saw until a few days ago, much less carried."

The Horus priest was standing with his back to Junipa, but she saw him tense. Death surged from every pore.

"All illusion," said Amenophis, "all masquerade. Like the gold on our skin." He ran a finger through the smudged gold paint on his face and rubbed it between his thumb and forefinger.

"The Empire is no illusion. It is real."

"Is it? Who will tell me, then, that it is not one of your illusions? There you're a master, Seth. Illusions. Masks. Sleights of hand. Others might have thought it was magic, but I know the truth. You explored the remains of the suboceanic kingdoms as a scholar. But the learned man has become a charlatan. You know how to influence the minds of men, how to delude them. Giant falcons and monsters, Seth, those are the toys of children but not the weapons with which one manages an empire. At least the sphinxes were right about that." The Pharaoh made a skipping turn and sank back onto the divan, back into the shadows. His weary voice floated into the darkness like a bird with a lame wing beat. "Is all this illusion? Tell me, Seth! Did you really awaken me to life or am I still lying in my burial chamber in the pyramid of Amun-Ka-Re? Have I really become the conqueror of the world, or is that only a dream you have conjured up for me? And is it true that all my loyal followers have left me and I am now all alone in a palace full of mummies—although perhaps I am one myself and have never left my grave? Tell me the truth, priest! What is illusion, and what is reality?"

Seth had not moved at all. Junipa moved slowly along the wall. She had a vague hope of making it to the door before one of the two of them noticed her.

"Do you really believe that?" asked Seth. Junipa stopped. Yet the words weren't directed to her, but to Amenophis. "Do you actually think that the events of the past forty years are nothing but an illusion?"

"I know what you are capable of," said the Pharaoh with a shrug. "Not real magic like the sphinxes, but you know all about deception. Perhaps in truth I am still laid out on the sandstone block in my pyramid, and you are standing beside me, your hand on my forehead—or whatever was necessary to plant all these images in my head. With every year that has passed and with every minute of the recent days my certainty has become greater: Nothing of all this is *true*, Seth! I am dreaming! My mind is caught in a huge, unique illusion! I have played the game, moved the pieces on the board, and had my fun. Why not? In truth, there was never anything to lose."

Junipa reached the door, slowly pressed down the gigantic latch. And yes, the high oaken door swung open! A draft of cool air came from the corridor and blew through her hair. But still she did not run away. The last meeting between the Pharaoh and his creator held her fast with a macabre fascination. She had to know what happened next. Had to see it.

Slowly Seth began walking up to the divan.

"Even my death is only an illusion," said Amenophis. From the mouth of a twelve-year-old, the sentence sounded as unreal as if he were rattling off a very complicated mathematical formula. Junipa was reminded again that the Pharaoh was much older than his body made him appear. Inconceivably older.

"Only illusion," he whispered once more, as if his thoughts were somewhere else, in a place of deep silence and darkness. In a grave, in the heart of a stepped pyramid.

"If that's what you think," said Seth, and he raised the sword and let it fall on the Pharaoh.

There was no resistance.

Not even a cry.

Amenophis died quietly and meekly. Seth, who had given him his life, took it from him again. Only a dream, the Pharaoh might think as he died, only delusion induced by the priest of Horus.

Junipa pushed on the door and slipped through the crack. Outside in the corridor she took four or five steps before she became aware of the silence. Seth wasn't following her.

Uncertain, she stopped.

Turned around. And went back.

Don't do it! her mind screamed. *Run away, as fast as you can!*

Nevertheless, Junipa stepped into the doorway and looked into the room again.

Seth was lying on the floor in front of the Pharaoh's body, his face turned in her direction. His left hand was clenched into a fist, the right loosening on the grip of the sword. The sickle blade was sticking out of his body. He had driven it into his own chest without a sound.

"He was wrong," he brought out with difficulty, spitting blood onto the parquet. "Everything is . . . true."

Junipa overcame her fear, her aversion, her disgust. Slowly she walked into the room and went to the divan and the two men who, until a few days before, had together guided the destiny of the greatest and cruelest realm in human history. Now they lay before her, the one dead in a sea of jaguar skins, the other dying at her feet.

"I am sorry," Seth whispered weakly, "because of the mirror—that was stupid."

Junipa went onto her knees and looked for words. She considered whether she should say something to lessen his pain or his disappointment. But perhaps that was just what he had done: He *had* lessened his pain. He had killed the master that he himself had created, had slain the child and the father.

It is good this way, she thought, and she had the feeling that the thought floated away like a feather. Like a last illusion.

Silently she stretched out a forefinger and stroked it over the strands of the golden network that was inlaid into Seth's scalp. It felt cool and not magic at all. Only like metal that had been pressed into flesh with terrible pain. It was exactly what it looked like: a network of gold in a place where it didn't belong.

As we are all, she thought sadly.

"Don't go . . . through the palace. The mummy soldiers are everywhere. There is no one left who . . . who controls them."

"What will they do?"

"I . . . don't know. Nothing, perhaps. Or . . ." He fell silent, began again: "Don't go. Too dangerous."

"I must find a mirror."

Seth tried to nod, but he wasn't able to. Instead, trembling, he stretched out a finger. Junipa looked in the direction he was pointing. And she saw what he meant.

Yes, she thought. *That could work.*

"Fare . . . well," Seth gasped.

Junipa fixed her eyes on his. "What for? You've destroyed everything."

Seth could not answer. His eyes dulled, the lids fluttered one last time. Then a slight shudder ran through his body and he stopped breathing.

Junipa walked wearily to the water basin beside the divan. It was big enough. She bent till her mouth was over it and whispered the glass word. Then she climbed onto the marble basin, swung her legs over the edge, and let herself down into her reflection.

The stone in her chest pulled her under.

9

SPHINX SPLINTERS

IT HAD NOT BEEN EASY.

Not easy at all.

Still, Merle had somehow managed to restrain Vermithrax before he could fly over the railing with a roar and tear the sphinx and the boy to pieces.

Now, much later, at the foot of the snow-covered stairs, the obsidian lion stopped and looked over at Lalapeya. The sphinx tilted her head, closed her eyes, and appeared to scent, the way Vermithrax sometimes did too, but in her it looked less like a wild animal. She does even that, Merle thought, with grace and beauty.

"Along there," Lalapeya said, and Vermithrax nodded. He'd come to the same conclusion.

What they both scented, Merle did not know. It was only after a while that she realized that it was the snow they were sensing, the way many animals instinctively flee an oncoming cold spell or store provisions in their burrows.

Some time had passed since the meeting on the staircase. Time in which Merle had to come to terms with the fact that the sphinx at her side was in fact her mother. And that it really was Serafin who was now sitting behind her on Vermithrax's back and had put his hands around her waist to hold on.

After the obsidian lion had understood that the sphinx on the stairs was not an enemy, he'd set Merle down on the steps. She and Serafin had fallen into each other's arms, to just stand there for a long time without words, hugging each other tightly. Merle had the feeling that he almost kissed her, but then his lips only touched her hair briefly, and all she could think of was that she hadn't washed it for days. It was crazy, really. Here they were, all trapped in this accursed sphinx stronghold, and she was thinking about washing her hair! Was that what being in love did to you? And then, *was* it being in love that was responsible for the lump in her throat and the fluttering in her stomach?

Serafin leaned close to her ear. "I missed you," he whispered. Her pulse raced. She was convinced that he must hear it, the hammering in her ears, the rushing of blood throughout her entire body. And if not that, then he doubtless felt the trembling of her legs, the trembling of every part of her.

She answered that she had missed him, too, which suddenly sounded trite and empty, she thought, because he'd said it to her first. Then she just talked straight on, said all sorts of other things, which two minutes later, thank heavens, she couldn't remember, because it was probably pretty incoherent. She was sure she sounded dumb and childish, and she didn't even know why.

And then, Lalapeya.

It was an entirely different kind of reunion from that with Serafin, most of all because it was, at least in Merle's view, not a real reunion. She had no memories of her mother, not her voice, not how she'd looked. She only knew her hands, from all the hours they had held each other's in the interior of the water mirror. But Lalapeya's hands were bandaged, and Merle couldn't touch them and reassure herself that they were the same hands she'd held before.

Not that, in all seriousness, she *had* to reassure herself. She knew that Lalapeya was her mother, knew it the moment she'd seen the sphinx on the stairs, even before she recognized Serafin on her back. That might simply have been due to appearances, to a resemblance of the eyes, a similar shape of face, or the long dark hair.

But it was far more that bound Merle to Lalapeya right off: The sphinx possessed exactly that degree of perfection that Merle sometimes imagined for herself, that beauty that she hoped she'd have when she grew up. But she was only fourteen, and a thing or two would happen in her face before it would become the firm, unchanging countenance she now saw before her above the slender shoulders of a sphinx.

She couldn't embrace Lalapeya because she was afraid of touching her injured arms, and she also wasn't sure it would be appropriate at their first meeting. So they only exchanged words. They spoke with a certain reserve, but also with scarcely concealed joy. Lalapeya was beaming despite her pain—and it was clear that she was feeling true happiness. And probably relief, too, that Merle didn't reproach her for what she'd experienced as a small child.

The Flowing Queen said not one word the whole time. Was simply silent, as if she were no longer a part of Merle. As if her spirit were already caught up in the battle with the Son of the Mother and had completely tuned out of its surroundings, even at a moment like this. Once Merle thought: She's hatching something. But then she told herself that the Flowing Queen possibly knew better than any of them what lay ahead. And then who could blame her if she didn't feel like talking?

It was Vermithrax who reminded Merle that they must be on their way. She then took great pains to explain their plan to Lalapeya and Serafin. Considering how much had happened since their last meeting, she quickly realized that she must limit herself to the most essential facts. Nevertheless she earned more than one incredulous look, and it took a while before she finally came to Winter's role in the whole story: who he was, what he was looking for, and why *they* were looking for *him*.

As they made their way down the stairs together, Serafin took over the story and told how they'd landed there. When he revealed that Eft, Dario, and the others were also in the Iron Eye, Merle could hardly believe it. Especially Dario! Her archenemy from the mirror workshop. But he'd been Serafin's antagonist even more than hers. If the two of them had now become friends, in fact, a whole lot must have happened. She burned to know the details.

"Eft is hurt," Serafin said. He told how she'd become involved in a fight with a sphinx guard at the foot of the stronghold. Eft had broken her lower leg, while Dario and Aristide had suffered severe sword cuts. None of their injuries were mortal, but after they'd tried to climb one of the staircases in the lower regions of the Eye together, the others had had to give up. Tiziano had stayed with them so that the injured weren't on their own, while Lalapeya and Serafin had continued the ascent. "I didn't want to leave them behind," he said finally, "but what were we supposed to do?"

"We could have turned around and gone back to the boat together," said Lalapeya. "But then it would all have been for nothing. So Serafin and I decided to go on alone."

"Where are they now?" asked Merle.

"In a library near the entrance," Serafin answered. "There's a gigantic library down there, incredibly huge."

Merle looked at him in disbelief. Until now she'd seen nothing but mirrors in the Iron Eye. Salons, halls, chambers of mirrors. The idea of one or even several giant libraries didn't fit into the picture she'd had of the fortress. She spoke her thoughts aloud.

Lalapeya looked over her shoulder. "To you, the sphinxes must seem a people of warriors and conquerors. You've never known them to be any different, in Venice with the Pharaoh or here. But the sphinxes are far more than that. They are a people of scholars. There are many wise heads among them, and once they gave the world great philosophers, storytellers, and playwrights. In the old desert cities there were theater arenas, where we gathered not only to watch, but also to discuss. Not all the sphinxes' arguments were carried on with weapons in those days. I can remember the great speeches, the clever debates and lectures—all at a time when the human race had more similarity to animals than the sphinxes do today. There were great minds among us, and then the artists . . . the old songs and poetry of the sphinxes possess a poetic charm that is unique."

"*She speaks the truth,*" the Flowing Queen said suddenly. "*In certain respects, anyway. However, humans were not so primitive and simpleminded as she claims.*"

Of course not, Merle thought acidly, or otherwise they'd hardly have made you into a goddess.

"I did not seek that out," said the Queen. *"It is characteristic of humans not to ask those whom they worship for permission first. And, unfortunately, it is also characteristic of the gods to grow accustomed to being worshipped."*

They were following a broad corridor a good two hundred yards wide with a high, curving ceiling, almost a kind of roofed-over street, though bigger and more imposing, when Vermithrax pointed forward with his head. "There! Do you see that?"

Merle blinked in the blinding white expanse of snowflakes, extended into a plain by the mirrors on both sides of the passage. The light was too bright for her to be able to make out anything in the distance. Serafin and Lalapeya didn't see what Vermithrax's sharp eyes had spied either.

"Sphinxes," he said. "But they aren't moving."

"Guards?" asked Lalapeya.

"Perhaps. Although I don't think that matters anymore."

The sphinx gave him an astonished look, while Merle gently scratched him behind the ear. "What do you mean?" she asked.

He purred briefly, perhaps because he enjoyed the touch, perhaps just to please her. "They're white," he said then.

"White?" Serafin repeated in amazement.

"Frozen to ice."

Merle felt Serafin's tension. He didn't like sitting inactive on the back of a lion and waiting. He itched to take matters into his own hands again. She understood him well; it didn't suit her temperament to become a victim of events either. Perhaps she'd let herself be pushed around too much since her meeting with the Queen, had done what was expected of her, not what she really wanted to. But at the same time, she had to recognize that she'd never had a choice: Her path had been predestined, and even at little crossings, a detour had been out of the question. Not for the first time she felt like a puppet who was being manipulated by everyone—worse yet, like a *child*. While basically, she never had been one. In the orphanage she'd had no time for it.

They went on, and soon Merle and the others, too, realized what Vermithrax had meant. Like a forest of statues, outlines detached themselves from the omnipresent white, hardly visible at first, then a little more clearly, finally as clear as polished glass. And in fact that's what the sphinxes resembled most: glass. Ice.

There were more than a dozen, fixed in various poses of fear and retreat. Some had tried to escape Winter's touch by running ahead of him; others had tried to fight, but the expressions on their faces showed the mood of despair, even of panic. Some had let the weapons slide from their hands, sickle swords half buried by the snow.

"What has happened here?" Lalapeya murmured.

"Winter was here," Merle said. "Everything he touches turns to ice. He told me that. Every living thing, with one exception—Summer. That's why he's looking for her. That's why they love each other."

There was a grating sound. Beside them, cracks went branching through the ice body of one sphinx, and a moment later he shattered with a crash into sharp-edged fragments. Only his four lion legs remained standing. They stuck out of the snow like road markers someone had forgotten.

For a moment none of them moved, as if they were turned to ice themselves. No one knew what had made the sphinx burst—until Serafin, cursing, pointed to a small dart that was sticking out of one of the pieces of debris.

"Someone's shooting at us!"

Merle scanned the passage, and she didn't have to look long before she discovered a sphinx who was leaning out of an archway and taking aim at them a second time. Before any of them could react, he fired. Lalapeya let out a scream as the shot grazed her shoulder and struck another ice sphinx behind her with a *clink*. Grinding and splintering, he broke apart.

More sphinxes appeared behind the sniper, but only some of them were armed. Some of them held chisels and hammers in their hands, as well as glass vessels and pouches.

They were going to examine the dead, Merle thought.

They would break off little pieces to examine them and look for a weak spot in their opponent.

Unfortunately, the troop of researchers was accompanied by several soldiers, who didn't look like the intellectual creatures Lalapeya had described before. They were big and muscular, with broad lion bodies and massive human shoulders.

Vermithrax took advantage of his wings and rose into the air with his riders. Lalapeya remained behind on the ground, but the obsidian lion had no intention of abandoning her. He rushed down onto the first adversary from above, knocked the bolt gun out of his hands, and struck him on the skull with his hind paw as he flew past. The sphinx was dead before he sank into the snow on bent legs.

The other soldiers reacted quickly: They shoved the sphinx researchers back under the arch, where they were protected from the lion's air attacks. One sprang forward and placed himself opposite Vermithrax, his sword raised, while another tried to reach the gun—obviously their only one.

Vermithrax rushed past the first sphinx—not even flinching when a sword blow bounced off his obsidian body, striking sparks—and knocked the weapon out of the sphinx's hand. The lion plunged down onto the second sphinx, seized him by the arms, pulled him high, and flung him against the mirror wall like a rag doll. The glass couldn't withstand the blow. The lifeless sphinx fell to the ground in a hail of silvery splinters and moved no more.

One of the researchers had used the opportunity to leap out of the protection of the archway and now raised the bolt gun. He was unskilled in handling weapons; his first shot whistled past Vermithrax a yard wide and punched a crack in the curved ceiling.

Meanwhile Lalapeya had hurried behind the ice statues toward the only possible path of flight: a low corridor that opened off the broad mirror street about thirty yards away. If she'd followed the street, she would have been a perfect target. She just had to break through the opening to the corridor, its lower half being blocked by a six-foot-high drift of snow. She pushed into it like a hill of flour: Powdery white exploded in all directions, and then she was out of sight.

Vermithrax flew a narrow loop under the ceiling. Merle, who was used to such maneuvers, screamed to Serafin to hold on to her tightly. He strengthened his grip with stiff, ice-cold fingers, while she did her best to clutch the glowing lion's mane. Serafin was slim and wiry, but he weighed quite a bit more than the featherweight Junipa. Merle wasn't sure how long she would be able to hold on. Her frost-stiffened fingers had lost their strength; in fact, she could hardly feel the mass of her limbs. The thick mane protected her from the cutting drafts, but that was a weak reassurance in the present situation. It was only a question of time before the two of them would tumble from Vermithrax's back and either break all their bones when they hit the ground or be spitted by one of the icy sphinx bodies.

"Did you see how many there are?" Serafin shouted into her ear over the wind and the rushing wings.

"Too many, anyway."

"But there aren't enough, are there?"

"What do you mean?"

"*I know what he is thinking,*" said the Queen, "*and he is right.*"

Serafin leaned closer to Merle, which was nice, even here, even now, and he brought his lips so close to her ear that they touched her hair. The tickling in Merle's belly increased, and that wasn't only because of Vermithrax's renewed flight of attack on the sphinxes. "Too few!" Serafin shouted again. "This is their stronghold, the most secure place of all for them. What's going on down there is destroying their world. And they only send a handful of soldiers and researchers?" Merle felt him shaking his head at her neck. "That doesn't make sense."

"Maybe," she said, "there aren't any more they can do without. It's the same reason you were able to walk into the fortress so easily."

"It wasn't *easy*," he contradicted.

Merle thought of the wounded, but nevertheless she argued, "Normally a few dozen guards would have been waiting for you, not just one. Or do you think the sphinxes would leave the Iron Eye as good as unguarded?"

Vermithrax killed a sphinx soldier with ease as he flew past him, like plucking a flower from a stem. Again the sickle swords of his adversaries struck sparks from his stone underside, but the tiny splinters they hacked out of his body didn't weaken him.

"They're too few," said Serafin. "That's just what I mean. Too few guards, and now too few to examine this catastrophe down there. It must be—"

"It must be," said Merle "that this isn't the only place in the Eye where something like this is happening!" Of course, Winter was skimming back and forth through the fortress on his search for Summer, exactly as he'd done in Hell. If he followed his courses over the world just as chaotically, it was no wonder that the seasons were so unreliable: Sometimes there was frost even in April, sometimes not, and you could never predict how the weather was going to be next week.

"The sphinxes have surely flocked here from all over the world to witness the Son of the Mother's return to life."

And Winter has come over them like a storm wind, Merle thought, and imagined gigantic salons full of ice sphinxes, like workshops of a crazed sculptor.

"It might have been that way."

Then Burbridge told Winter about it! Merle thought. He planned for Winter to pass through here as revenge on the sphinxes.

"And the Stone Light?"

Burbridge must somehow have managed to take Winter into the mirror room.

"Looks very much like it."

This isn't the first time all this has happened, is it?

"No. But that was perhaps not Winter. Possibly Summer freed herself that time, or someone or something else came to her aid."

The downfall of the suboceanic kingdoms!

"And the Mayas. The Incas. Atlantis."

Merle recognized none of these names, but their very sound made her shudder. While Vermithrax detached himself from the sphinxes and flew up to the passageway into which Lalapeya had vanished, she explained her conjecture to Serafin, as well as she could in the headwind. He agreed with her.

They pulled in their heads as Vermithrax swept through the low arch, whirled up the remains of the snowdrift with his claws, and finally set himself down on all fours. The passage was too narrow to fly very far. Moreover, Lalapeya was waiting for them, looking worried. Her eyes sought Merle, saw that she was uninjured, and then turned to Vermithrax. "How many are there?"

"Four left. At least. Perhaps a few more."

"There must have been an army."

"Indeed."

Merle held back a grin, but she knew that they all had

the same thought. Considering how effortless Vermithrax's fight with the sphinxes had been, Winter must have already taken a large part of the work from him.

The lion and the sphinx hurried along the passageway side by side, as their adversaries appeared in the opening behind them. The scientists had stayed behind, and two soldiers took up the chase. At their backs, on the mirror street, a deep alarm signal sounded several times: The sphinx researchers used horns to call other troops from the breadth of the Iron Eye.

"Do you know your way around here?" Vermithrax asked the sphinx.

"No. When I left my people to watch over the lagoon, there was no Iron Eye yet. The sphinxes had always been a people of the desert and of the deep caves. All this here"—she shook her head resignedly—"all this has nothing to do with what I once knew."

Although the same cold prevailed in the corridor as everywhere in the Iron Eye, the snow cover around them became thinner after a few steps, finally disappearing altogether. Cutting winds blew against them, but the winds brought no new ice. Nevertheless the mirror floor was slippery with frozen dampness, and neither Vermithrax nor Lalapeya got on as quickly as they wished. The obsidian lion could have stood against their two pursuers and in all probability vanquished them, but he feared that the two would soon be followed by a larger number of opponents. And as long as he was involved in fights, he couldn't protect Merle and Serafin from attackers.

A new passageway crossed theirs, and to the right, still more sphinxes were approaching. After a quick look, Vermithrax hurried straight on. The sphinxes couldn't miss his glow. There was no question of a hiding place, especially as there were hardly any doors, only open archways that led into broad halls, infinite rooms in this imitation of the mirror world.

They crossed open canals with frozen surfaces and filigreed bridges that appeared about to break but didn't even tremble as the weighty obsidian lion thundered across them. They came through a hilly landscape of mirror shards, waste dumps as high as houses of silvery chips and sharp pieces, and then steps went down again, and more steps, and still more steps.

The pursuers stayed on their trail the whole time, often concealed behind curves and corners, but always present as surges of noise: a tramping of lion feet on ice, a roaring of angry voices, a jumble of savage curses and commands.

And then again they were stumbling through high snow, damper and heavier than before, so high that Vermithrax sank up to his belly and Lalapeya was hopelessly stuck after a few steps. The obsidian lion swept the snow masses to the side with his wings, but it soon turned out that he couldn't get them any farther that way.

"Vermithrax," cried Lalapeya, "can you carry a third rider?"

"Two or three more, if there's room for them. But that doesn't help us much."

"Perhaps it does." And as she spoke, a change took place in her.

Merle looked on with open mouth and wide eyes, while Serafin took her hand reassuringly. "Don't worry," he whispered, "she does that a lot."

Around Lalapeya, yellow fountains of sand appeared to shoot up from the snow where her lion legs were stuck. They enveloped her in seconds, until she dissolved in them, as if her entire body had exploded in an eruption of desert dust. Just as quickly the tiny particles joined together again, and Lalapeya emerged from them. She was unchanged from the hips up, but now she had long, slender human legs, which were bare, despite the cold. The fur jacket she'd gotten from the pirates reached down to her thighs, but her lower legs were exposed to the snow without protection.

Serafin let go of Merle and slipped backward a little. "Quick, up here!" he called.

Lalapeya fought her way through the snow to them, and Merle and Serafin pulled her onto the lion between them. The sphinx couldn't use her injured arms, and if she stood much longer in the snow in her bare feet, the same thing would happen to her legs. Serafin pushed as close as possible against her, put his arms around her to Merle, and yelled, "Let's go!"

Vermithrax rose from the ground and shook the snow from his paws. He dashed away over the ice, only several yards from the mirrored roof. The walls were barely far enough apart for his gigantic wings, but somehow he succeeded in not hitting the tips and carried his riders safely over the snow. Their pursuers were left behind as they tried to stomp their way through the high snow and then had to give up.

With a triumphant roar Vermithrax shot out of a round opening at the end of the tunnel into an unevenly higher hall, where it was still snowing out of gray fog that hung beneath the ceiling like real winter clouds. The flakes were thick and fluffy. They immediately stuck to Vermithrax and his riders and drove into their eyes. The lion's glow was garishly reflected in the falling snow, like curtains of gleaming light. The visibility extended for a few yards only.

"I can't see anything!" Vermithrax lurched in flight and sneezed once, so hard that Merle was afraid the shaking would throw them all from his back. Whatever his bath in the Stone Light had done, it hadn't made him immune to colds.

The obsidian lion was having trouble maintaining his altitude. He was as good as blind in the snowstorm, and the wet snow weighed down his wings. "I have to go down," he cried finally, but they'd all realized long ago that this move was unavoidable.

They sank down with the snowflakes, deeper and deeper, but the bottom they were expecting didn't appear. What they'd taken for a hall was in reality a mighty chasm, an abyss.

"Up ahead there!" Merle yelled through the deluge of snow. Snow got into her mouth. "A bridge!"

A narrow footbridge of mirror glass spanned the infinite emptiness like a guitar string. It was hardly more than forty inches wide and had no railings; both ends lay buried in the snowstorm somewhere.

Vermithrax flew down to it, and with full confidence in the sphinxes' architecture, he landed on it. It gave a slight shudder but no sign at all that the construction wouldn't bear his weight. On both ends of the bridge, five or six yards of the snow edges loosened and tumbled into the whitish gray deep.

Vermithrax shook his wings to shake off the lumpy layer of ice that had impeded his flying. Serafin tried to pull the ends of his coat wide enough to cover Lalapeya's bare legs, but she waved him off.

"Let me down. I can walk on my own again here. Vermithrax won't be flying anymore in this snow, anyway."

"The path is too narrow," said Serafin. "If you get off Vermithrax sideways, you'll fall down into the chasm."

"What about from behind?"

Serafin and Merle looked over their shoulders at the same time. The sight of the abyss on both sides of the pathway was alarming. As a master thief, Serafin had balanced over Venice's roofs all year long without wasting more than a thought on the danger. But this was different. If he went into a slide on the wet, slushy snow, nothing could save him, not luck, not skill.

"I'll try it," he said.

"No," Merle contradicted. "Don't be silly."

He looked past Lalapeya to Merle. "Her legs will freeze if she doesn't change back. So she *must* get down."

Merle glared at him: as if she didn't know that herself. Nevertheless, she was afraid for him and Lalapeya. Although, after watching her transformation, the thought that the sphinx actually was her mother seemed even more incredible.

"Be careful," said Lalapeya as Serafin slowly slid backward.

"*Plucky,*" the Flowing Queen commented dryly.

"Just hold still!" Serafin called to Vermithrax. His voice sounded grim. Merle held her breath.

"Don't worry," replied the lion, and in fact he did not move a fraction of an inch. Even his heartbeat, which Merle could feel clearly beneath her legs most of the time, appeared to stop.

With infinite caution, Serafin slid backward over Vermithrax's hips. At the same time he grasped the lion's tail;

it gave him additional stability when his boot soles sank into the snow. For a long moment he swayed slightly and cast mistrustful glances into the abyss to the right and to the left. Finally he gave Lalapeya the sign to follow him. His feet seemed to swim in the loose slush, so uncertain was his footing on the bridge. An overhasty movement and he would slide over the edge along with a gigantic snow clump.

He let go of the lion's tail in order to free the way for Lalapeya. She nimbly slid back and off the lion, while Merle twisted her neck and worriedly watched what was going on behind her.

"They will make it," said the Queen.

Easy for you to say, Merle thought.

"Take one step back," said the sphinx to Serafin, "but carefully."

Extremely carefully he moved backward, striving not to pay any more attention to the depths below him.

"Good," said Lalapeya. "And now sit down. And support yourself with your hands."

He did that. He felt sick and dizzy, master thief or not. Only when he was sitting somewhat securely in the snow did he dare take a deep breath.

Lalapeya changed into a column of whirling sand, from which, in a flash, came flesh and hair and bone. After the sphinx was standing there in her lion form again, she told Serafin to climb onto her back. He obeyed, and the color returned to his face. It reassured him a little that Lalapeya and Vermithrax had four legs that gave them more traction up here. They had their predator's genes to thank that the suction of the abyss had no power over them. Fear of heights was alien, not only to the winged Vermithrax but also to Lalapeya, as was any clumsy or superfluous movement.

Merle gave a shudder of relief when Serafin was finally sitting safely on Lalapeya's back. For a long moment she'd even forgotten the cold, which was troubling her more and more. Now she again felt the bite of the frost, the icy burden of the snow, and the severe tugging of the high wind.

"What now?" asked Vermithrax.

"We follow the path," Merle suggested. "Or does someone have a better idea?"

They moved forward on eight lion paws, not sure what to expect on the other side of the thick blizzard.

After a few steps, Vermithrax stopped again. Merle caught sight of the obstacle at the same moment.

A figure crouched in front of them on the narrow band.

A man sitting cross-legged.

His long hair was snow-white, his skin very light, as if someone had formed the motionless figure of snow. The man had his head thrown back, his closed eyes facing upward. His bony hands were clutched around his knees, the dark blue veins standing out clearly.

"He's meditating," said Lalapeya in amazement.

"No," said Merle softly. "He's seeking."

Winter dropped his head and looked over at them wearily.

10

THE ONLY WAY

IT ALMOST SEEMED AS IF HE'D BEEN WAITING FOR THEM. "Merle," he said, sounding neither pleased nor annoyed. "She's here. Summer is here."

"I know."

Vermithrax had come within two paces of him.

"Don't come any closer," said Winter. "You'll all freeze to ice if you touch me."

"You killed the sphinxes," Merle said.

"Yes."

"How many are left?"

"I don't know. Not enough to oppose me."

"Do you know where they've hidden Summer?"

He nodded and pointed down into the chasm.

"Down there?" Merle was irritated to have to pull every word out of him.

Again a nod. Only then did she notice that the thick snow made a detour around him. No ice crystals caught in his hair, no flakes stuck to his white clothes. His breath didn't even come from his lips in puffs of white. It was as if Winter himself was no part at all of the season he embodied.

"I've come this far," he said, "but now I lack the power to take the last step."

"I don't understand."

"Summer is being held at the bottom of this shaft. There are no other entrances, I've searched everywhere."

"So?"

Winter smiled shyly and very vulnerably. "How am I supposed to get down there? Jump?"

She'd had the idea that of course a being like him would be able to fly if he needed to. But he could not. He'd frosted the Egyptians and the Iron Eye with a new ice age, but he wasn't able to advance to the bottom of this shaft.

"How long have you been sitting there?"

Winter sighed. "Much too long."

"*He is a whining weakling,*" grumbled the Flowing Queen. "*And all this uproar he is causing around him does not change that.*"

Don't be so unfair, Merle thought.

"Pah! A weakling." Had the Queen had a nose, she would probably have wrinkled it. *"How long can he have been here? He left Hell shortly before us."*

He's just . . . well, sensitive. He's exaggerating.

"Sensitive? He is a liar! If he succeeded in getting from the pyramid to here in the delta in such a short time and then still managed to breeze through the Eye and freeze hundreds of sphinxes . . . that is damned fast, is it not?"

Merle glanced back over her shoulder at Serafin and Lalapeya. Both were looking impatient but also uncertain, faced with the strange creature blocking their way.

She turned to Winter again. "You really can't fly?"

"Not down there. I ride on the icy winds and the snowstorms. But that's meaningless here."

"What do you mean?"

Again he sighed from the bottom of his heart while the Queen uttered an exaggerated groan. "I'll explain it to you, Merle," he said. "And to your friends if they want to hear it."

Serafin growled something that sounded like, "What else can we do?"

"Summer is at the bottom of this shaft. Her strength, her sun heat, if you will, normally rises up through the shaft. No man can approach the ground, he'd burn up in an instant."

Merle shifted her weight nervously and looked down from Vermithrax's back into the deep. She saw nothing but whitish gray chaos. And she was getting colder and colder, quite terribly now.

"My presence here in the shaft interrupts the flow of heat," he continued. "Ice and fire meet each other down there, about halfway between me and her. The snow instantly melts in the air, the cold transforms into heat. Sometimes there are thunderstorms when we meet. I could let myself be carried down there by the icy winds, but Summer is captive and doesn't have her heat under control. She is weakened and not able to cool herself down, as she usually does when we meet. Down there, the wind would turn into a lukewarm puff of air, the ice would melt, and I . . . well, imagine a snowflake on a hot plate." He buried his bony face in his hands. "Do you understand now?"

Merle nodded uncomfortably.

"Then you grasp the utter hopelessness of my situation," he proclaimed, waving his arms.

"That might not even be true," said the Queen venomously. *"This fellow has almost annihilated an entire people, and now he is sitting here crying!"*

You could easily show a little more sympathy.

"I cannot bear him."

You were certainly not everyone's darling among the gods.

"Ask him if he has ever heard the word dignity.*"*

That I most certainly will not.

"I could do it for you."

Don't you dare!

Serafin interrupted them. "Merle, what now? We can't just keep standing here forever."

Of course not, she thought with a shiver.

Then Vermithrax spoke up. "I know a solution."

In the tense silence, only the Queen murmured sourly, *"Whatever it is, it had better be quick. We have no more time. The Son of the Mother is awake."*

"I can fly down there and try to free Summer," Vermithrax said. "I'm stone, heat and cold can't affect me . . . at least I think not. Besides, I've survived a bath in the Stone Light, so I'll probably survive here as well. When Summer is free, I can carry Winter to her. Or her to him."

Merle's fingers clutched his mane even more tightly. "That's out of the question!"

"It's the only way."

Merle felt that the Queen was about to take command of her voice, but she pushed her roughly back. For the last time, she snapped at the Queen in her mind, back off!

"He will endanger everything if he does that! Without him we will not get far."

You mean, if he doesn't do what you say, don't you?

"It is not about that."

Oh, yes, that's exactly what it's about, thought Merle. You've used him, just as you've used me. You knew from the beginning that we were coming here, that we had no other choice. You've always brought us exactly where you wanted us. "And now that's the end of it!" She said the last words out loud, and everyone looked at her in puzzlement. Her face had turned red, and the heat felt almost comfortable in the ice-cold air.

"She doesn't like the idea," Vermithrax stated.

Merle shook her head grimly. "At the moment what she thinks doesn't count."

The lion turned to Winter. "What will happen when Summer is free?"

The albino made a dramatic gesture with his hands that took in the entire Iron Eye. "What always has happened. All this will lose its power. Exactly as before."

Merle pricked up her ears. "Like the suboceanic kingdoms?" Her guess was very close to the mark.

Winter nodded. "They weren't the only ones to have tried it, but their failure was the most spectacular." He thought for a moment. "How shall I explain it? They tap her strength, the strength of the sun—perhaps that describes it the best. They don't realize that they are only injuring themselves. They know of the failure of the old ones, but they try it again anyway. They are so terribly weak, and they think they are so infinitely strong." Winter shook his head. "These fools! They cannot win, one way or the other. They will destroy themselves, sooner or later, even if we do not free Summer."

"But what do they want?" asked Serafin. "Why are they doing all this?"

Lalapeya answered him. "They are using Summer to

drive the barks, the factories, and the machines with her energy. Thus they have helped bring the Pharaoh to power and conquered the world. But this world was really only a finger exercise for them, only a plaything. What is actually important to them is somewhere else."

"All the mirrors?" Merle whispered.

"Their plan is to tear down the barriers between the worlds with the Iron Eye. With their fortress they're going to move from one world to another and carry on an unprecedented campaign of conquest."

Vermithrax growled. "But that takes magic. More magic than that of an ordinary sphinx."

"The Son of the Mother," said Merle. The coming events were unreeling in her mind like the light and shadow play of a magic lantern. "*He's* the key to the whole thing, isn't he? When he awakens, the Stone Light will take control. And the Iron Eye will move through the mirror world in order to smash the gates to the other worlds." She envisioned the gigantic fortress appearing in the labyrinths of the mirror world and destroying thousands upon thousands of mirror doors. The chaos in the worlds would be indescribable. Under the direction of the Light, the sphinxes would travel through the worlds like a mob of freebooters and sow death and destruction, exactly as they'd done in her own world. In other places too they would not dirty their own fingers but help upstarts like the Horus priests and Amenophis to power. Others would do the work for them, while they sat in their fortress and waited. A people of scholars and poets, Lalapeya had said. The sphinxes *were* artists, scientists, and philosophers, but the price for their life of literature and debate was a high one. And its cost was supposed to be paid by entire worlds.

"Merle," said Vermithrax firmly, "go to your mother."

She still hesitated, even though she felt that he had made his decision. "You must promise to come back."

Vermithrax purred like a kitten. "But of course."

"Promise!"

"I promise you."

That wasn't much reassurance, maybe nothing but empty words. Nevertheless, she felt a little better.

"*Just fool yourself,*" said the Queen nastily. "*You humans always were the greatest at that.*"

Merle wondered why the Queen was being so unbearable. Perhaps because Vermithrax's plan was better than her own: free Summer, thus rob the last sphinxes of their power, and so hinder the awakening of the Son of the Mother.

And the Queen's plan? Why didn't she reveal it? Where was the catch? For there was a plan, Merle had no doubt of that.

"*I am worried about him.*" The Queen's tone had changed abruptly. No more sarcasm, no bitter irony. Instead, real concern. "*I want to speak with him—if you will allow it.*"

"Yes," Merle said, "of course." The Queen played with

her feelings as if she were a piano, knew exactly which keys she had to press when. Merle saw through her and still could do nothing against it.

"Vermithrax," said the Queen in Merle's voice. "It is I."

Serafin and Lalapeya stared at Merle, and she had to remind herself that the two knew her story, of course, but they were hearing the Queen *speak* from Merle's mouth for the first time. Vermithrax had also pricked up his ears.

"I must tell you something."

Vermithrax cast an uncertain look at Winter, who had raised himself and stood astride the path, without swaying, even without blinking. "Now, Queen? Couldn't it wait?"

"No. Listen to me." He did, and all the others did as well. Even Winter tilted his head as if he were concentrating entirely on the words that fell from Merle's lips and yet were not her own. "I am Sekhmet, the mother of the sphinxes," the Queen went on, "that you know."

At least for Lalapeya and Serafin, that was a surprise. Lalapeya was going to say something, but the Queen interrupted her: "Not now. Vermithrax is right, haste is needed. What I have to say concerns only him. After I bore the Son of the Mother and with him generated the sphinx people, I soon recognized what had happened: The Stone Light had deceived me. And it had used me. I placed compliant servants in the world for it. When it became clear to me what that meant, I decided to do something. I could not kill all sphinxes and make everything unhappen—but I could keep the Son of the Mother from being made into the slave of the Light. I fought with him, mother against son, and finally I succeeded in defeating him. I was the only one who had the power to do that. I killed him and the sphinxes buried him in the lagoon." She paused, hesitated, and then continued: "What happened then, you know. But my story does not end with that, and it is important that you learn it now. You most of all, Vermithrax."

The lion nodded thoughtfully, as if he already guessed what was coming.

"I knew that I could not watch the lagoon alone, and so from the stone of the image the humans had erected in my honor, I created the first stone lions. I created them of magic and my own heart's blood, and I think that makes them—like the sphinxes and yet entirely different from them—my children, does it not?"

The lion, unable to look Merle and the Queen in the eye as they sat on his back, lowered his head. "Great Sekhmet," he whispered humbly.

"No," the Queen exclaimed, "it is not about honoring me! I intend only that you know the truth about the origins of your people. No one remembers anymore when and how the stone lions came to be in the lagoon, and so I am telling you. The lagoon is the birthplace of the stone lions, for after the Son of the Mother was buried there, I created you as guards: I myself would watch over him, but I needed helpers, my arms and my legs and hands and claws. Thus arose the first of your people, and after I was sure that you were equal to the task, I gave up my own body and became the Flowing Queen. I could not and would not live as a goddess anymore with the shame of what I had done. I became one with the water. On the one hand that was the proper decision, but on the other it was a mistake, for with it I gave up supervision of the stone lions. My servants were strong, but at the same time trusting creatures, who got mixed up with humans." She hesitated before she went on in a bitter tone, "You know what happened. How the humans betrayed the lions and robbed them of their wings; the flight of those who escaped the treachery; and finally Vermithrax's unsuccessful attack on Venice to redress the wrong that had been done to his ancestors."

The obsidian lion was silent. He'd listened with lowered head. He and his companions were the children of Sekhmet. The stone guards of the Son of the Mother.

"Then it is right that I am here today," he said finally, lifting his head with new determination. "So perhaps I can make up for the mistake of my forefathers. They failed to guard the Son of the Mother."

"Just as I did," said Lalapeya.

"And I," said the Queen from Merle's mouth.

"But fate has given me a chance," Vermithrax growled. "Perhaps all of us. We failed then, but today we have another chance to stop the Son of the Mother. And I will be no lion if we do not succeed." He uttered a pugnacious growl. "Merle, get down now."

She obeyed, very slowly, very carefully, until Lalapeya enveloped her in her injured arms. But Vermithrax walked up to Winter. The albino touched him on the nose, scratched under his chin. Vermithrax purred. He'd been right: The frost had no effect on his stone body.

"Good luck," said Merle softly. Serafin bent down from the back of the sphinx and placed a hand on Merle's shoulder. "Don't worry," he whispered, "he'll manage it."

Winter nodded to Vermithrax one last time; then the lion let out a battle roar and leaped into the deep. After a few yards, his wings stabilized his flight, and a few moments later he was only a glowing phantom behind a curtain of ice and snow. At last he faded entirely, like a candle flame extinguished in white wax.

"He will manage it," whispered the Queen.

And if he doesn't, Merle thought. What will become of us then?

Ignoring her bandaged arms, Lalapeya embraced her daughter even more tightly and looked her in the eyes at close range.

And thus they stood for a long time, with no one saying a word.

Vermithrax felt it, he felt the Stone Light in him and yet knew that it could not harm him. He'd been able to feel it when he'd bathed in the Light, down there under the dome of Axis Mundi—nothing tangible, no clear sensation. But he'd known that there was something in him that protected him from the Light and at the same time united him with it. Now it was clear to him that it was the legacy of Sekhmet, the foremother of all stone lions and sphinxes, the Flowing Queen. She had been touched by a beam of the Stone Light, and a little of this contact had also passed over to the lions. When he'd plunged into the Light, it had recognized itself in Vermithrax and protected him. Even more: It had made him stronger than ever before. Perhaps involuntarily, but that no longer mattered.

He was Vermithrax, the biggest and most powerful among the lions of the lagoon. And he was here to do what he'd been born for. If he were to die doing it, it would only close the circle of his existence. And if Seth had told the truth, he was anyway the last of his people, the last of those lions who could fly and speak. The last free creature of his species.

He propelled himself downward with broad sweeps of his wings, flew down with the snowflakes, overtook them, shot like a comet through the middle of them into the abyss. Soon it seemed to him they were growing smaller and wetter, no longer the fluffy flakes of farther up but slushy dots, then drops. Snow turned to rain. With the onset of heat, the water evaporated too, and he entered a zone of comfortable warmth, then heat, then finally roaring fire. The air around him shimmered and boiled, but he inhaled it the same as the icy air of the high heavens, and his lungs, glowing like everything in him, sucked out the oxygen and kept him alive.

He was proven right. The Light, which had made him strong, at the same time protected him from heat and cold.

Soon it was so hot that even stone would melt to glass, yet his obsidian body withstood it. The distant walls of the shaft had long since become unrecognizable; whatever material they might be made of, it was also not of this world. Of magic mirrors, perhaps, like the rest of the Iron Eye. Or of pure magic. He understood little of these things, and they didn't interest him. He only wanted to carry out the tasks he had undertaken. Free Summer. Defeat the sphinxes. Stop the Son of the Mother.

Then he saw her.

Until now he'd not been aware that he'd almost reached the floor of the shaft It might just as well have been a lake of fire, even more flames in this sea of heat. But the light was pure and natural, not like that one of stone that spun its net of meanness and greed in Hell. This light was the one that bore warmth, the light in whose beams Vermithrax's lion people had sunned themselves on the rock terraces of Africa.

The light of the summer.

There she lay, stretched out in a sea of glitter and flame, supported by hot air, floating over the floor like a fruit just waiting to be picked.

There were no guards, no chains. Both would have been incinerated in a second. All that held her down here and had placed her in a trance was the sphinxes' magic.

Vermithrax held himself above the floating Summer with gentle strokes of his wings and gazed down at her for a long moment. She looked as if she could be Winter's sister, tall and thin, almost bony. She didn't look healthy, not in the human sense, but that might lie in her nature. Her hair was of fire. Flames also flickered behind her eyelids, yellow and red like glowing coals. Her lips were as silky as flower petals, her skin pale, her fingernails sickles of pure fire.

She didn't have her heat under control, Winter had said. And in fact everywhere there was fire licking out of her body, her body itself seemed to waver and melt like a wax figure in the heat of August.

Vermithrax observed her a moment longer. Then he stretched out his left front paw and touched her with the greatest imaginable gentleness on the upper thigh.

His heart stopped racing.

He knew about her heat, yet he didn't *feel* it.

The Light, he thought again. *The Stone Light is protecting me. I should be grateful to it and to that accursed Burbridge.*

He pulled his paw back, waited for two or three breaths, then began a narrow loop around Summer's floating body, past the flickering fountain of her fiery locks. Her hair streamed out like an explosion of fireworks, forever frozen in time. Once, twice, he kept circling around her until he was sure that he had cut through the invisible bands of the chain spell. Then he floated cautiously beside her and tried to lift her from her bed of heat.

She lay light as a feather between his forepaws and detached from her float with a slight jerk, as if he'd pulled a nail off a magnet. At the same moment the brightness around her dimmed, the shimmering of the air faded, the surroundings grew sharper. The heat ebbed perceptibly, he could literally see it. No one, no sphinx had thought it would ever be possible that there'd be a creature who could get to her here. The Stone Light, the power *behind* the power of the sphinxes, had deprived itself of the victory.

Vermithrax rose slowly upward, clutching Summer's thin body firmly. She looked undernourished, a little like Merle's friend Junipa. But with Summer it was not a sign of too little food or illness. Who could say how a season should look, her skin, her features? If Winter was a healthy example of his kind, then probably there was nothing wrong with Summer's body.

Her mind, however, was another matter.

Although Vermithrax had severed the bonds of the sphinx spell, Summer still showed no signs of awakening. She hung in his grasp like a doll, not moving. He wondered if her eyelids were at least fluttering, as is often the case with humans who are gradually awakening from unconsciousness. But Summer was *not* human. Anyway, during the steep flight it was hard for him to lift her far enough away to be able to see her face.

They flew in an aura of warmth. The snow around them melted and gradually tapered off, the closer they came to the dizzying narrow path where Winter and the others awaited them. The power of the two seasons mutually canceled out, now that Summer was no longer hurling all her power to the outside. Vermithrax assumed that this was a sign of her recovery: Her body was again using its energy on herself, directing its power inside, endeavoring to heal.

They'd almost reached the thin bridge over the mirror abyss when Summer moved in Vermithrax's claws. She groaned softly as life gradually returned to her.

Now he flew even faster, turned a triumphal pirouette around the bridge, and let Summer glide into Winter's out-stretched arms. While the two embraced—he stormily, she barely conscious, still a shadow of herself—the obsidian lion sank down and gently landed in front of Lalapeya.

The sphinx let go of Merle, and Vermithrax enjoyed it when the girl threw herself on his neck with a happy shout, buried her face in his glowing mane, and wept with relief. The boy on the sphinx's back was grinning broadly. Vermithrax winked at him, seeming extraordinarily human as he did so.

Summer was growing more alert with every second in Winter's embrace. When she opened her eyes, they'd taken on the colors of sun-glowing desert sand. The flames in her hair went out. Her narrow hands clutched

Winter's back, and she let out a sob. "It happened again," she whispered. She was now weeping quite openly, without any shame. Winter's closeness gave her support.

Vermithrax looked over at Merle, who had detached herself from him. Yet it was Serafin who put words to the question they all had: "And was that really all?"

For a moment there was silence. No more snow fell, and the winter winds around them had died down almost entirely. They stood quietly over the abyss, whose floor shone like a sea of silver below them.

"No," said Merle, and again it was the Flowing Queen who spoke out of her. "That was by no means all."

"But—" Serafin was interrupted when Merle shook her head and the Queen said, "It has happened. The sphinxes have used Summer's last energies and reached their goal."

"The Son of the Mother?" asked Vermithrax somberly.

"Yes," said the Queen through Merle's mouth. "The Son of the Mother is awake. I feel him, not far from here. And now there is only one who is a match for him."

As there had been once before. Like that other time.

Mother against son, son against mother.

"Sekhmet," said Merle waveringly, now again the mistress of her own voice. "Only Sekhmet can still stop her son. But for that—" She hesitated and sought dazedly for words, which she really already knew, because the Queen had passed them to her. "She says that for that she needs her old body."

11

THE SON OF THE MOTHER

IT BEGAN WITH A SUNBARK THAT FELL FROM THE SKY somewhere over the Mediterranean. It plunged down like a dead bird struck by a hunter's shot from ambush. The golden sickle wobbled downward in narrow spirals, and the sphinx on board could do nothing to stop the dive. The bark splashed into the sea in the center of a foaming fountain. Salt water sprayed through the viewing slits and leaky weld joints from all sides. Seconds later it had vanished.

Elsewhere, similar scenes took place over land. Sunbarks full of mummy soldiers fell out of the clouds and smashed on bare rocks, on deserted fields, between the tips of deep forests. Some fell over cities, frequently in the midst of burned-out ruins, or onto the roofs of houses, inhabited or uninhabited. Some sank in swamps and broad marshes, others were swallowed by jungles or desert dunes. High in the mountains they scraped along steep walls and were torn apart on rock projections.

Where men and women were witness to the events, they broke into jubilation, without guessing that the cause of it all was a girl and her motley companions in distant Egypt. Others suppressed their joy out of fear of the mummy soldiers who were guarding them—until they noticed that a change was also taking place in them.

Everywhere in the world, mummies disintegrated into dust and dried limbs, to stained corpse flesh and rattling tools. In some places it was a matter of a few breaths, during which whole peoples were instantly freed of their oppressors; elsewhere it took hours until the last mummy soldier became a lifeless corpse.

Sphinxes tried to hold the workers in their mummy factories in check, but they were too few, most of them having long since left on the road to the Iron Eye. Nor were there any Horus priests, who might have stopped the downfall; Amenophis himself had wiped them out. As for the human servants of the Empire, their number was too small, their will too weak, and their strength too little to offer serious resistance to the flaring rebellion.

The Egyptian Empire that had taken decades to establish perished within a few hours.

On the borders of the free Czarist kingdom, it wasn't long before the defenders on the walls and palisades, in the trenches and on the towers of lonely tundra fortresses, knew the truth. They dared raids, which quickly turned into campaigns—campaigns against an enemy who suddenly wasn't there anymore, against crumbling mummy bodies and shattered sunbarks.

In many places the mighty collectors, the dreaded flagships of the Empire, plunged out of the clouds. Some into bleak no-man's-lands, a handful over cities. Some took hundreds of slaves to death with them, all extinguished by a single stroke of Fate.

Here and there a few sphinxes tried vainly to keep their flying apparatus in the sky, mustering all their sphinx magic. But their attempts were to no avail. Those who crawled from the smoking, bent steel wreckage alive were killed by their human slaves. Only a few succeeded in finding shelter in woods and caves, with no hope of ever again being able to walk safely in daylight.

The world changed. Not stealthily, not timidly. The change was like a thunder bolt out of the blue, a flash in the darkest night. What was suppressed and destroyed over decades broke out like a flower through ashes and stone, developed shoots, stretched and extended itself, bloomed to resistance and new strength.

And while life awakened anew on all continents, the snow in the Egyptian desert melted.

Winter stayed behind with Summer on the edge of the abyss, where the path ran into the wall of mirror-polished steel. Summer was still too weak to help Merle and the others in their battle.

Merle was clutching Vermithrax's mane tightly with both hands. The obsidian lion bore her swiftly through the arched passages, halls, and stairwells of the Iron Eye. Water ran down the walls around them, snowdrifts and icicles melted into streamlets and lakes.

Serafin sat behind Merle, while Lalapeya followed them through the mirrored corridors at a fast gallop.

"And is she sure," Serafin shouted into Merle's ear, "that her body is preserved somewhere in the fortress?"

"She said that."

"And she also knows where?"

"She said she sensed it—after all, it was once part of her."

The Queen spoke up again. *"That ill-bred boy talks about me as if I were not here."*

And you aren't, either, Merle retorted. At least not for him. How much farther do we have to go?

"We shall see."

That's not fair.

"I know just as little as you. The presence of my former body fills all the lower floors of the fortress, exactly like the

presence of the Son of the Mother. They must both be very nearby."

Things were coming to their conclusion—*a* conclusion. Merle had to admit that everything had gotten to be too much for her long ago. So much had happened since Seth had abducted Junipa in the mirror room, and for a long time she'd felt unable to make sense out of anything anymore. Yet Serafin and the closeness of Vermithrax and Lalapeya gave her a vague feeling of security. She wished that Winter had stayed at her side too. But he refused to leave Summer and had sunk into his own superhumanity again. The seasons would continue to exist, no matter what became of the world, which they would continue to cover with ice and heat and fall foliage. Vermithrax had risked his life for Summer, but no one thanked him for it. Merle was angry at Winter. They could have used his help—whatever the Queen was planning.

You do have a plan, don't you? she asked in her mind, but as usual with inconvenient questions, she received no answer.

As they went along they passed crystallized sphinxes, frozen to milky ice when Winter touched them during his wanderings through the fortress. Water dripped onto the mirrored floor from their bodies. Merle couldn't shake off the feeling that she'd been moving through a gigantic mirrored mausoleum for hours.

Serafin was having the same thoughts. "Very odd," he said as they passed a group of icy sphinx bodies. "They're our enemies, of course, but this . . . I don't know. . . ."

Merle understood what he was trying to say. "It feels wrong somehow, doesn't it?"

He nodded. "Maybe because it's always wrong when so many living creatures simply stop *being*." After a pause, he added, "No matter what they've done."

Merle was silent for a moment, thinking about what he'd said. She came to an upsetting conclusion. "I'm not sorry for them. I mean, I'm trying . . . but I can't be. I'm simply not sorry for them. Too much has happened for that. They have millions of human beings on their consciences." She'd almost said "billions," but her tongue hesitated to put the truth into words.

The frozen sphinx bodies whisked past them like a procession, forming bizarrely columned halls of ice cadavers. Broad puddles had already formed around some of them. The thaw created by the reunion of Summer and Winter was spreading into the lower stories.

Lalapeya had been silent the entire time. Merle couldn't get rid of the feeling that her mother was observing her, as if she were trying to make a picture of her daughter that went beyond the simple surface. As if her eyes were also examining Merle's interior, her heart. Presumably she was listening to every word that Merle said.

"*Now I know!*" the Queen burst out. "*I know why my body and the Son of the Mother are overlapping this way. Why it is so difficult to keep them separate.*"

And?

"They are both here."

In the fortress? But we've known that for a long time.

"Silly girl! In one single place. In a hall." A short silence, then: *"Directly in front of us!"*

Merle was about to warn the others, but she didn't need to. Vermithrax stopped suddenly as a knife-sharp outline emerged from the panorama of mirrors and ice, a horizontal line—they were approaching the edge of a wide balcony. And beyond it, again . . . an abyss.

The lion slowly felt his way forward, Lalapeya at his side.

"What is that?" Serafin whispered.

Merle could only guess the answer: They had stumbled on the heart of the Iron Eye, on the temple of the lion goddess.

Sekhmet's shrine. The crypt of the Flowing Queen.

Merle and Serafin leaped off Vermithrax's back and, on their knees, made their way to the edge. Serafin's hand moved over Merle's. She gave him a smile and enclosed his fingers in a firm grasp. Warmth crept up her arm, electrifying her. Unwillingly, she tore her eyes away to look down into the deep emptiness below.

On the opposite wall of the hall—for a hall it was, even if its proportions were beyond comparison with any human work of construction, any throne room, any cathedral—stood the gigantic statue of a lioness, taller than Venice's

Basilica of San Marco. It was stone, with predator's fangs bared, each tooth as long as a tree trunk. Her gaze looked dark and mean, the eyes sunk in deep shadow. On each of her claws, hewn from rock, was spitted the figure of a human, as casually as dirt between her paws.

The statue was reflected many times in the mirror walls of the temple, over and over, so that it seemed as if it were not a single statue of Sekhmet standing there but a dozen or more.

"*That* was you?" Merle exclaimed.

"*Sekhmet,*" contradicted the Queen dejectedly, "*not I.*"

"But you're one and the same!"

"*We were once.*" Her tone was bitter. "*But I was never as the sphinxes have represented me. When I was still called Sekhmet, they revered me as a goddess—but not as that* thing *there!*" There was loathing in her voice now. "*Since then they have apparently made a demon of me. Look at the dead in the claws. I have never killed humans. But it fits with their plans. 'Sekhmet did it,' they say, "so we can do it too.' That is the way it is with all gods who can no longer defend themselves—their adherents shape them just as it suits them. In time, no one looks for the truth anymore.*"

"This must be the deepest point of the Iron Eye," Serafin said. "Look down there."

From all the entrances to the mighty mirror temple, streams of water were splashing and gurgling into the hall, some only small rivulets, some as wide as brooks.

234

Lalapeya cautiously bent a little farther forward and looked down over the edge of the drop-off. "This is all going to be flooded soon, when the snow in the upper levels is completely melted."

Vermithrax was still unable to take his eyes off the tower-high stature. "Is *that* her body?"

At first Merle had had the same thought, but now she knew better. "No, only a statue."

"Where is her proper body, then?"

"*Over there,*" the Queen said in Merle's head. "*Look to the right, past the front paws. You see that low altar? And what is lying on it?*"

Merle strained and blinked and tried to make something out. It was far away. The floor of the hall lay deep below them; the balcony ran around the upper third of the wall. Whatever the Queen intended, they could reach it only with Vermithrax's help.

Merle discovered the altar just as she was about to give up. She also saw the body that was lying on it. Stretched out on its side, with the four paws pointed toward them. A wild cat. A lioness. She was no bigger than an ordinary animal; on the contrary, she appeared to Merle much more delicate, almost fragile. Her surface was gray, as if it were dusty—or stone.

Merle pointed out her discovery to the others.

"She's made of stone," Vermithrax purred. He sounded as if he felt a little flattered.

"I was not always," said the Queen with Merle's voice so that all could hear her. "When I laid aside that body, it was of flesh and blood. It must have turned to stone over all the millennia. I did not know that."

"That could be due to the touch of the Stone Light," said Lalapeya thoughtfully.

"Yes," agreed the Queen. "Possibly."

Serafin was still holding Merle's hand. He looked back and forth from her to the slender lion body far below. It seemed to him that with every moment the gurgling was a little louder, stronger, angrier. Not all the openings in the walls were at floor level; some, like the balcony, lay dozens of yards high, and the water plunged into the space below with tremendous force. The ice on the ledge where they stood was also melting, surrounding them all with slush and shallow puddles. Here and there it was already dripping over the edge into the depths below.

"We must go down there." The Queen's voice sounded somber and ominous. And once more Merle became aware that she was hiding something from her. The last part of the truth. Perhaps the most unpleasant.

Just tell me, she demanded in her head, what is it?

The Queen hesitated. *"When the time comes."*

No! Now!

The hesitation lengthened, became stubborn silence.

What's wrong, damn it? Merle tried to sound as demanding as possible—which wasn't so easy when you were only saying the words in your head and not with your mouth.

"We cannot call everything into question now."

No one's even talking about that.

"Please, Merle. It is already hard enough."

Merle was going to argue when Serafin tugged on her hand.

"Merle!"

She whirled around tensely. "What is it?"

"Something's not right down there!"

"Absolutely not," Vermithrax agreed.

Lalapeya said nothing. She was stiff with horror.

At first everything seemed unchanged: the gigantic statue of the demonic Sekhmet; next to it, much smaller, her lifeless body on the altar; and everywhere around them the water, flowing down out of the halls and passages of the Iron Eye and covering the floor.

No new arrivals. No sphinxes far and wide.

The mirror images! The reflections of the powerful statue had begun to move. At a fleeting look it might have been because of the curtains of water that streamed down the walls and broke up and distorted the reflections. But then gentle quaking and trembling turned into loud thundering. Gigantic limbs tensed and stretched. A titanic body awakened from its rigidity.

Merle felt as if she were falling miles deep into a chasm of silver. Everything around her whirled for a moment, faster and faster. She felt sick with dizziness. Only gradually did the truth emerge from the whirlpool of impressions.

Some of the reflections were in fact from the statue, and those continued motionless. But the rest reflected a being that had only the size and part of the lion body in common with the statue.

Serafin's hand clutched Merle's fingers. He'd seen this creature once before, when the Egyptian collector's magic had pulled it from the wreckage of the cemetery island of San Michele.

The Son of the Mother—the largest of all sphinxes, hideous and misshapen like a distorted image of all those who revered him—had been in the temple the entire time. In front of the wall, seen at a distance, he had appeared to be one of the innumerable mirror images.

Now they knew better.

"Down!" whispered Lalapeya sharply. "He hasn't noticed us yet!"

All followed her direction. Merle's joints had turned to ice. Vermithrax had raised the obsidian hairs of his mane in excitement and extended all his claws, ready for the last, the greatest of all fights.

Maybe the shortest.

What gave the sphinxes refined, almost perfect looks, in the Son of the Mother looked displaced, crooked, distorted. The sphinx god measured some dozen yards from his muscular human chest to his lion hindquarters. His hands had grotesque, knotted fingers, and many too many of them; they looked almost like spiders' bodies and were big enough to mash Merle and her companions with one blow. His claws were yellow and did not retract. With every step they punched a row of three-foot-deep holes in the temple's mirror floor. The four lion legs and the two human arms were too long and had too many joints, bent and stretched by muscle cords that lay strangely wrong under pelt and skin, as if the Son of the Mother had far more of them than any other sphinx.

And then his face.

The eyes were too small for his size and glinted with the same light as that of the Stone Light. His cheekbones were unnaturally prominent, and in the wings of his nose were cavelike nostrils. His forehead resembled a steep wall of furrows and scars, stemming from forgotten battles long ago. The teeth behind the scaly lips were a wall of stalactites and stalagmites, the entry to a stinking grotto, whose puffs of breath took form as crimson clouds. Only his hair was silky and shining, full and long, and of the deepest black.

Merle knew that they were all having the same thought: There was no point in it anymore. Nothing and no one could stand against such a creature. Certainly not the delicate lioness who lay lifeless down there on the altar.

"I had forgotten how dangerous he is," the Queen said tonelessly.

Marvelous, thought Merle bitterly. Just exactly what I wanted to hear.

"*Oh,*" responded the Queen hastily, "*I can beat him! I have already done it once.*"

That was pretty long ago.

"*You are quite right there.*"

The Queen appeared to have lost some of the optimism she'd displayed recently at every mention of the battle with the Son of the Mother. The Queen was daunted, whether she wanted to admit it or not. And deep inside Merle felt a fear that was not her own. The Flowing Queen was afraid.

"What's he going to do?" whispered Vermithrax with a dry voice.

The Son of the Mother was pacing back and forth in front of the grotesque statue of Sekhmet, sometimes faster, sometimes skulking, like a hunter circling his prey. His gaze was directed toward the tiny body at the feet of the statue, the petrified lion cadaver, which seemed to disquiet him far more than the masses of water that would soon overflow the mirrored temple.

"He doesn't know what to do," Lalapeya whispered. She had pushed her bandaged hands to the edge of the balcony. She must be in pain, but she didn't show it. "Just look how nervous he is. He knows he must make a decision, but he doesn't dare to take the last step."

"What last step?" Vermithrax asked.

"To destroy his mother's body," said Serafin. "That's why he's here. He wants to erase Sekhmet for all time, so that he doesn't fare again the way he did the last time."

"*Yes,*" said the Flowing Queen to Merle. "*We must hurry.*"

Merle nodded. "Vermithrax, you must take me down there."

The obsidian lion raised a bushy eyebrow. "Past him?"

"We have no choice, do we?"

The Flowing Queen had still not said a word about how she was going to change back into her own body from Merle's. But now, like an unexpected stroke of lightning, Merle realized that obviously that was where the Queen's last secret lay. That was what she had concealed from her the whole time.

Good, Merle thought, the time has come. Tell me.

She had the feeling that for the first time, the Queen was searching for words. Her hesitation became unbearable.

Hurry up, will you!

"*When I leave you, Merle . . .*" She stopped, stuck.

What then?

"*When I leave your body, you will die.*"

Merle was silent. Thinking nothing. Suddenly there was only emptiness in her.

"*Merle, please . . .*" Again hesitation, longer this time. "*If there were another possibility somehow . . .*"

Her consciousness was swept away. No thoughts. Not

even memories, things to feel sad about. No omissions, no unfulfilled wishes. Nothing.

"I am sorry."

Agreed, Merle thought.

"What?"

I agree.

"Is that all?"

What did you expect? That I'd scream and rage and defend myself?

A moment of silence, then: *"I do not know what I expected."*

Perhaps I even suspected it.

"You did not."

Yes, perhaps.

"I . . . oh, damn it."

Explain it to me. Why can't I live without you?

"That is not it. It is not the change that is the reason. It is rather that . . ."

Yes?

"It is true that I can leave your body without your being harmed. If I move from one living creature to another, that is not a problem. But Sekhmet's body is dead, you understand? It has no life of its own anymore. And therefore—"

Therefore you must take one with you.

"Yes. Something like that."

You intend to revive that stone corpse down there with my strength.

"There is no other way. I am sorry."

You knew that the whole time, didn't you?

Silence.

Didn't you?

"Yes."

Serafin pressed her hand again. "What are you two talking about?" His eyes were filled with concern.

"Nothing." Merle thought it sounded hollow and empty. "It's all right."

At the same moment the Queen took control of her voice and before Merle could stop her, she said, "The others have a right to know. They shall decide."

"Decide what?" Serafin straightened up mistrustfully. Lalapeya also shifted closer. "What do you mean?" she asked.

In vain Merle concentrated, trying to push back the Queen's voice, as she had once before, in Hell. But this time she was unsuccessful. She could only listen as the Queen explained to the others through her mouth what was going to happen. Must happen.

"No," whispered Serafin. "That can't be."

"There must be another way," growled Vermithrax, and it sounded almost like a threat.

Lalapeya inched over to Merle and embraced her. She was going to say something, had already opened her lips, when a light, girlish voice exclaimed, "You can't be serious!"

Merle looked up. She couldn't believe it. "Junipa!"

She detached herself from Lalapeya and Serafin, slithered

as quickly as she could away from the balcony edge through the snow and water, finally leaped up, and enclosed Junipa in her arms.

"Are you all right? Are you hurt? What happened?" For a few moments the words of the Flowing Queen were forgotten, just as her own fate was. She couldn't let go of Junipa, had to keep staring at her like a ghost who'd appeared in front of her from nowhere. "Where's Seth? What did he do to you?"

Junipa smiled shyly, but she seemed to be trying to conceal pain that was tormenting her. The grip of the Stone Light. The invisible claws that were stretching toward her heart.

The Son of the Mother continued to tramp back and forth in the hall below. He was much too deep in his hate-filled thoughts to notice the goings-on up on the balcony. And he was still hesitant to destroy the body of his mother. His heavy breathing and snorting echoed back from the walls, and the cracking and shattering of the mirror floor under his claws sounded like icebergs splitting as they bumped together.

Vermithrax was making an effort to keep his eye on the beast. But at the same time he kept looking over at the two girls. Serafin also crept away from the mirror edge to the others, gave Junipa a quick hug, and then turned to her four companions, who'd appeared behind her. The entire group had walked out of a mirror wall, on which the last ice patterns were gradually melting.

Serafin greeted Dario, Tiziano, and Aristide. Dario and Tiziano were supporting Eft, whose right leg was emergency-splinted with a piece of wood; it looked as if someone had hacked it out of a bookcase with a blade, like an oversized splinter. Eft was pressing the lipless edges of her mermaid mouth firmly together. She was in pain, but she wasn't complaining.

"She insisted on coming to you," explained Junipa, who'd noticed Serafin's look. "I found her and the others in a library."

Merle gave the mermaid a warm smile over Junipa's shoulder. For a moment the surroundings were overlaid by a scene from the past, a gondola ride at Eft's side through a night-dark tunnel. "You have been touched by the Flowing Queen," Eft had said that time. "You are something very special."

Merle shook off the image and turned to Junipa again. "What happened with Seth? I was so worried about you!"

Junipa's face darkened. "We were in Venice, Seth and I. We were with the Pharaoh."

"With the—"

Junipa nodded. "Amenophis is dead. And the Empire has collapsed."

"Has Seth—"

"Killed him, yes. After that he killed himself. But he let me go."

The Queen roused in Merle's mind. *"The sphinxes abandoned Amenophis. That is just like them! They used the Empire to awaken the Son of the Mother. And now they want to move on. They are not content with this one world."*

Junipa grabbed Merle by the shoulder. "You weren't really serious before, were you? What you said . . . or *she* did. Whoever."

Merle shook off her hand with a jerk. Her eyes avoided Junipa's mirror gaze, slipped past her to the others. She felt as if she'd been driven into a corner from which there was no escape.

"Without the Son of the Mother, the sphinxes have no power to leave our world," she said, now turning to Junipa again, but still trying not to meet her eyes. "And if there is only one way to beat him . . . I have no choice, Junipa. No one here has."

Junipa shook her head in despair. "That's not you talking!"

"The Queen wanted all of you to know the truth, so that you could make the decision for me. But now I'm the one who is speaking. And I won't allow someone else to decide. This is my affair alone, not yours."

"No!" Junipa seized her hand. "Let me do it, Merle. Tell her she can change into me."

"What nonsense!"

"Not nonsense." Junipa's gaze was firm and full of determination. "It won't be much longer until the Stone

Light gains power over me again. I can feel it. It feels around and pulls on me. I don't have much more time."

"Then go through the mirror into another world. The Light will have no more power over you there."

"I will not allow you to die. Look at me. My eyes aren't human. My heart isn't human. I'm a joke, Merle. A mean, bad joke." She looked over at Serafin, who was listening very carefully to her every word. "Anyway, you have him, Merle. You have something to live for. But I? When you're dead I have no one left."

"That is not true," said Eft.

Merle wrapped her arms tightly around Junipa, pressing her friend to her as hard as she could. "Look around you, Junipa. These are your friends. None of them will let you down."

Serafin stood there, torn. There must be another possibility. There simply *must*.

"But you heard her," Dario chimed in. "The Pharaoh is dead. That's all that matters. The Empire is as good as defeated. And if the sphinxes really want to get out of here, so much the better for us. Why should they make out any better in other worlds than in ours? We survived, didn't we? Others will also survive. That isn't our affair. And not yours either, Merle."

She sent him a sad smile. She and Dario had never liked each other, but now it touched her that even he was trying to dissuade her from her decision. Serafin had done the right thing when he'd ended hostilities with Dario: Dario wasn't a bad fellow. Even if he didn't, couldn't, grasp what she had to do.

"*We have no more time*," said the Flowing Queen. "*The Son of the Mother will soon overcome his reluctance and destroy my body. Then it will be too late.*"

Merle released Junipa. "I must go now."

"No!" Junipa's mirror eyes filled with tears. Merle had thought Junipa couldn't cry at all.

Merle reached into the pocket of her dress and pulled out the magic water mirror. She turned around and handed it to Lalapeya. "Here, I think this is yours. The phantom in it . . . promise me to let him go, if you get out of here safely."

Lalapeya took the mirror in her bandaged hands. Her eyes were fastened on her daughter. "Don't do it, Merle."

Merle embraced her. "Farewell." Her voice threatened to choke on her tears, but she had them quickly under control. "I always knew that you were there somewhere."

Lalapeya's face was pale and tight. She couldn't believe that soon she would again lose the daughter she had just found. "It's your decision, Merle." She smiled nervously. "That's the mistake all parents make, isn't it? They don't want to accept that their children can make their own decisions. But the way it looks, you leave me no other choice."

Merle blinked away her tears and hugged her mother

one last time. Then she walked over to Eft and the others, said good-bye to them as well, again avoided Junipa's unhappy eyes, and finally went over to Serafin.

In the background, the Son of the Mother snorted and scraped in the depths of the mirrored temple. His raging sounded ever more furious, ever more impatient.

Serafin took her in his arms and gave her a kiss on the forehead. "I don't want you to do this."

She smiled. "I know."

"But that doesn't change anything, does it?"

"No . . . no, I guess not."

"We should never have gone into that house that night. Then all this wouldn't have happened."

Merle felt the warmth that he was giving off. "If we hadn't saved the Queen from the Egyptians . . . who knows what would have happened. Perhaps then every-thing would be looking even worse."

"But we would have had each other."

"Yes." She smiled. "That would have been lovely."

"I don't give a damn about the rest of the world."

Merle shook her head. "You do so, and you know it. Not even Dario meant what he said before. Maybe now. Maybe even tomorrow morning. But sometime he's going to think differently about it. Just like you. Pain goes away. It always does."

"Let me go," he said urgently. "If it's possible for the

Queen to cross over into me, then she can take my life strength to awaken her body."

"Why should I say yes to you if I said no to Junipa?"

"Because . . . because then you can be there for Junipa. She's your friend, isn't she?"

She smiled and bumped her nose against his. "Nice try." Then she kissed him lightly on the lips, just very quickly, and pulled away from him.

"What he says is right, Merle," the Queen said dejectedly. *"I could cross over into him and—"*

No, thought Merle, turning around to Vermithrax. "It's time to go."

The lion's huge obsidian eyes were glistening. "I will obey you. To the end. But you should know that this is not my wish."

"You don't have to obey me, Vermithrax. I'm just some girl. You do agree to it, don't you? You know that I'm right." Vermithrax, too, had once been ready to sacrifice himself for his people. If anyone at all could understand her, he could.

He lowered his head sadly and said nothing. Merle climbed onto his back and stretched to catch a look over the edge into the chasm. She watched the Son of the Mother walk slowly up to the statue. He neared Sekhmet's laid-out body and scratched his claws more powerfully. Under the water surface the mirror floor had shattered to stars of silver glass.

Merle looked around at the others one last time as

the lion went up to the edge and unfolded his wings.

Junipa was staring up at her, weeping. She looked as if any moment she was going to run to stop Vermithrax. Merle smiled at her friend and gently shook her head. "No," she whispered.

Eft struggled to straighten up in the grasp of the two boys, disregarding her broken leg. That she, who'd been born without legs, should be put out of action by an injured leg was perhaps the most cruel twist of fate.

The boys, too, were looking sadly at Merle. Dario had his jaws tightly clenched, as if he were grinding iron with his teeth. Tiziano blinked and fought unsuccessfully against a single tear that ran down his cheek.

Lalapeya appeared strangely blurred, as if her body were caught in the transformation between human and sphinx. She did not take her eyes off her daughter, and for the first time Merle really felt that Lalapeya was no longer a stranger, no distant hand inside the water mirror. She was her mother. She had finally found her.

Vermithrax reached the edge of the balcony. His wings rose and fell twice in succession, as if he had to try first to see if they would obey him.

"*It is time*," said the Queen in alarm. "*He is about to destroy my body.*"

Vermithrax's front paws left the floor.

Behind them someone screamed Merle's name.

On the bottom, the Son of the Mother noticed the

movement out of the corner of his dark eyes. He turned around and caught sight of the obsidian lion on the edge. A primeval bellow broke from his throat, making the mirrored walls tremble and the water on the floor churn.

Serafin sprinted behind Vermithrax. Just as the lion was about to rise into the air, Serafin also pushed off, landed with both palms on Vermithrax's rear end, and was somehow able to grab hold of his fur and pull himself up. Suddenly he sat swaying behind her. "I'm coming along! No matter where—I'm coming along!"

The Son of the Mother screamed even more loudly as Vermithrax dove steeply at him, despite the second rider on his back. It was too late for him to turn around now that the beast had become aware of them. They could only bring it to an end as quickly as possible. Somehow.

"You're crazy!" Merle yelled over her shoulder while they sped downward in a nosedive.

"That's why we suit each other, isn't it?" Serafin yelled in her ear. He could hardly make himself heard over the rushing air and the roaring of the masses of water. The world sank into noise and attack and flickering silver.

Vermithrax raced toward the Son of the Mother's mighty skull. Compared to it he was as small as an insect and yet an impressive sight, bathed in the lava glow of the Stone Light and roaring with determination and explosive energy.

High over them the others crowded to the edge of the balcony and looked down into the abyss. Their faces had taken on the color of the ice that was melting around them. It no longer mattered if the Son of the Mother caught sight of them. Whatever might happen, they no longer had any influence over the events.

The gigantic sphinx took a step back from his mother's statue, turned completely around, and stretched his open jaws toward Vermithrax. His screeching made the heart of the Iron Eye quake; the high mirror temple shook to its foundations. The water on the floor boiled and surged like a witch's cauldron. The monster's movements were astonishingly fast, considering his size, and it was clear that he would become even more dangerous when he finally regained his old dexterity. He had lain for millennia in the depths of the lagoon; at the height of his powers he would probably have killed Vermithrax with one blow.

The obsidian lion avoided the many-fingered claws and raced toward one of the walls until Merle could recognize herself and Serafin in the mirror. They grew larger and larger and finally whistled past, a garish spot of color, as Vermithrax swerved sharply in front of the wall and flew back again. The sphinx bellowed and raged. He tried to swat them out of the air like an annoying mosquito, but time after time he grabbed emptiness. Vermithrax's flying maneuvers took Merle's and Serafin's breath away, but they enabled him to outfox the Son of the Mother.

The deeper they flew, the more dangerous it became. Here the beast not only tried to catch them with his fingers but also with his powerful lion paws. Once Vermithrax was left no choice but to fly between his towering legs. They escaped the monster's long claws by only a hair's breadth. The Son of the Mother struck and kicked at them, fountains of water sprayed up and splashed around them, and the beast's angry screaming hurt their ears.

Vermithrax re-emerged on the other side of his body, near enough to the stone image of Sekhmet to be able to fly down in its shadow and, on the back side of the statue, find safety for himself and his riders from their adversary's overgrown paws and sickle-sharp claws.

"Let me get down," Merle cried into Vermithrax's ear. "I'll manage it on foot just as well. You draw him away."

Vermithrax obeyed and sank to the ground in the protection of the statue. Merle slid from his back into the meltwater, and Serafin jumped down behind her. The swirling floods were horribly cold and reached up to their knees. For a moment the chill took their breath away.

There was no time for a farewell—already shattering blows were striking the mighty statue. The Son of the Mother had finally lost any respect and on the other side was doing his best to make the statue fall. Merle wondered if perhaps he guessed what they were up to.

"*Of course,*" said the Flowing Queen. "*He can feel me, just as I do him. But he has not been back in the world of the living long enough. His feelings confuse him. He still cannot control them. Yet he feels the danger. And soon he will be his old self again. Do not let yourself be deceived by the spectacle he has just created. He is no simple-minded colossus, quite the contrary. His intelligence is sharp. When he stops behaving like a newborn, he will become* really *dangerous."*

Vermithrax winked sadly at Merle one last time. Then he shot around the side of the statue and flew toward the Son of the Mother in quick zigzags, even more daringly now, ready to sacrifice himself so that Merle could reach her goal unhindered.

She looked around and saw the altar on which Sekhmet's petrified body lay, about thirty yards away, by the side of the statue. There they would be unprotected and open to the attacks of the Son of the Mother. But if their plan worked, Vermithrax's utterly mad maneuvers would distract him from Sekhmet as well as from her.

Serafin waded through the water beside her as they sneaked along the statue's stone feet. "Please, Merle—let me do it."

She didn't look at him. "Do you think I came this far in order to turn it over to someone else all of a sudden?"

He held her back by the shoulder, and against her will she stopped, after a last look at Vermithrax, who was skillfully luring the Son of the Mother in another direction. "This isn't worth it," he said darkly. "All of this . . . it doesn't pay to die for this."

"Let it be," she replied, shaking her head. "We have no more time for that."

Serafin looked up at Vermithrax and the sphinx colossus. She saw what was going on inside him. His powerlessness was written in his face. She knew exactly how that felt.

"Ask the Queen," Serafin tried one last time. "She can't want you to die. Tell her she can have me in your place."

"It would be possible," said the Queen hesitantly.

"No!" Merle made a motion with her hand as if she wanted to wave off any further argument. "That's enough. Stop it, both of you."

She tore herself loose and now ran as fast as she could, through the water to the stone Sekhmet. Serafin followed her again. Both no longer paid any attention to the fact that the Son of the Mother had only to turn around to discover them. They were betting everything on one card.

Merle reached the altar and leaped up the few steps. Again she was astonished at how delicate Sekhmet's body was, a simple lioness, with scarcely any resemblance to the demonic goddess that the builders of the statue had made of her. She wondered who had been allowed to enter this temple and regard the true Sekhmet. Certainly only a narrow circle of initiates, chosen priests of the sphinxes, the most powerful of their magicians.

What must I do? she asked in her thoughts.

"Touch her." The Queen hesitated a moment. *"I'll attend to everything else."*

Merle closed her eyes and laid her palm between the stone ears of the lion goddess. But at the same moment

Serafin seized her lower arm, and for a second she believed he was going to stop her, if necessary with force—but he did not do that.

Instead he pulled her around, took her in his arms, and kissed her.

Merle did not resist. She had never kissed a boy, not like that, and when she opened her lips and their tongues touched, it was as if she were someplace else with him, in a place that was perhaps as dangerous as this one was, only less final, less cold. In a place where hope could take the place of despair.

She opened her eyes and saw that he was looking at her. She returned the look, looked deep inside him.

And recognized the truth.

"No!" she cried and pushed him away, confused, shocked. Incapable of believing what had just happened.

Queen? she shouted in her thoughts. Sekhmet?

She received no answer.

Serafin smiled sadly as he bowed his head and took her place beside the altar.

"No!" she cried once more. "That can't—you didn't do that!"

"He is a brave boy," said the Flowing Queen with Serafin's voice. With *his* mouth, with *his* lips. "I will not let you die, Merle. His offer was very courageous. And in the end the decision was mine alone."

Serafin placed his hand between the ears of the petrified body.

Merle leaped at him, intending to tear him away, but Serafin only shook his head. "No," he whispered.

"But . . . but you . . ." Her words faded. He had kissed her and given the Flowing Queen the opportunity to move into his body. He had really done it!

She felt her knees buckling. She sank down hard on the highest altar step, only an inch above the water.

"The change has weakened you," said the Queen and Serafin together. "You will sleep for a while. You must rest now."

She wanted to pull herself up again, to rush to Serafin again, to beg him not to do it. But her body no longer belonged to her, as if along with the Queen had also gone the strength that had kept Merle on her feet for days at a time, almost without sleep and food. Now exhaustion came over her like an insidious illness. It left Merle no trace of a chance.

Reality slid away from her, shifted, blurred. Her voice failed, her limbs could no longer bear her weight.

She saw Serafin standing before the altar with eyes closed.

Saw Vermithrax circling around the head of the raging Son of the Mother like a lightning bug.

Saw her friends up on the parapet, small as knitting needle heads, a chain of dark shadow beads.

Serafin swam before her eyes. All her surroundings dissolved. And then suddenly she saw his face before her, very pale, his eyes closed.

Her spirit cried out, in infinite pain and grief, but no sound crossed her lips.

A gray phantom whisked away above her, the feather-light spring of a predatory cat of gray stone. Water splashed. Waves struck against her cheeks.

Sekhmet, she thought.

Serafin.

The end of the world inside her, perhaps also around her.

The Son of the Mother. Sekhmet. And over and over again, Serafin.

She must sleep. Only sleep. This battle was no longer hers.

Hands seized her, growing out of the silver mirror of the water surface. Thin girls' hands, followed by others. Figures everywhere in the water.

Serafin lived no more. She knew it. Wanted it not to be true. Knew it nevertheless.

The screams of the Son of the Mother everywhere around her.

"Merle," whispered Junipa, and pulled her into the mirror world.

Darkness. Then silver.

No more screams.

"Merle." Still Junipa's whisper.

Merle tried to speak, to ask something, but her lips only trembled, her voice faded to a croak.

"Yes," said Junipa gently, "it's over."

12

SNOWMELT

SOMEONE HAD LIFTED HER ONTO VERMITHRAX'S BACK.
Someone was sitting behind her and holding her firmly.
Serafin? No, not he. It must be Eft. With her broken leg,
she couldn't walk.

Junipa was guiding them through the mirror world.
She went ahead, followed by Vermithrax, who held the
two riders on his back with his folded wings. His heart
was racing, he was panting with exhaustion. Merle had
the feeling he was limping, but she herself was too weak
to say for certain. She looked wearily over her shoulder.
Behind the lion walked Lalapeya in her sphinx form.

Dario, Tiziano, and Aristide brought up the rear.

Something lay across Lalapeya's back, a long bundle. Merle couldn't quite make it out. Everything was hazy, and she felt as if she were in a dream. What she never would have thought possible had happened: She missed the alien voice inside her, someone who gave her courage or argued with her; who lectured her and gave her the feeling that her mind and her body were not exhausted. Someone who questioned her, kept her alert, who always and constantly challenged her.

But now she had only herself.

Not even Serafin.

At that moment she knew what Lalapeya bore on her back. It was no bundle.

A body. Serafin's corpse.

She thought of his last kiss.

Only much later did Merle realize that their path through the silvery labyrinth of the mirror world was a flight. Those who could walk were hurrying—in front of them all, Junipa, who gained in strength and determination in this place, at last free from the Stone Light again.

As if she were in a trance, Merle thought back to that day she and Junipa had entered the mirror world for the first time. Arcimboldo had opened the door for them so that they could capture the annoying phantoms in his mirrors. Junipa had been uncertain, afraid. There was no sense of that now. She moved along the secret mirror paths as if she belonged here, as if she'd never known anything else.

Around them, again and again, individual mirrors went dark, like windows in the night. The glass in some shattered, and a cold, dark suction pulled at those hurrying past. In some passages it was as if a black shadow were eating up the walls, as one mirror after another turned dark. Some exploded as Vermithrax ran by them. Tiny shards poured over the comrades like star splinters.

The longer they were under way, however, the more rarely the mirrors burst. The memory of the dark chasms faded, and soon there were no more signs of the annihilation that lay behind them. All around them shone pure silver, flickering in the light of the places and the worlds that lay beyond them. Junipa slowed, and the entire group with her.

Merle tried to pull herself upright, but she sank forward into Vermithrax's mane again. From behind she felt Eft's hand on her waist, holding her firmly. Merle heard voices: Junipa, Vermithrax, Eft. But she understood nothing of what they said. In the beginning they'd still sounded frantic, excited, almost panicked. Now their words were quieter, then fewer, until finally all lay in deep silence.

Merle tried to look around once more, to Serafin, but Eft would not allow her to. Or was it only her own lack of strength that held her back?

She felt that her mind was fading away again, that the pictures were becoming fuzzy again, the sounds of their steps duller and farther away. When someone spoke to her, she didn't understand what was said.

Was that a good thing?

She didn't even know an answer to that.

They buried Serafin where desert had once been.

Now the broad fields of sand were drinking the melt-water, the dunes dissolved into mud, and the yellow-brown ravines became streambeds. How long would that go on? Nobody knew. It was clear that the desert would change. As would the entire country.

Egypt would become fruitful, Lalapeya maintained. For those who had resisted the Pharaoh and survived his reign of terror, this was the chance for a new beginning.

Serafin's grave lay on a rock projection, where the sand and water had bonded to firm bog. When the sun shone again and evaporated the dampness, he would be as secure here as if glass had been poured around him. The rock overlooked the desert, many miles wide in all four directions. From here one looked up and out at the blue-green ribbon of the Nile, which was still the source of all life in Egypt, and someone, perhaps Lalapeya, said it would be good that Serafin began his last journey from this place.

Merle hardly listened, although many words were spoken on this day when they took leave of Serafin. Each who had witnessed his sacrifice said something; even Captain Calvino, who'd barely known Serafin, gave a short speech.

The submarine lay at the Nile bank, securely moored in front of a palm grove, or what the frost had left of it.

Merle was the last who walked to the grave, a pit that Vermithrax had dug out of the mud with his claws. She went down on her haunches and looked for a long time at the cloth in which they'd wrapped Serafin. Utterly quiet, utterly stunned, she had taken her leave, or tried to at least.

But the true leave-taking would last months, years perhaps, she knew that.

Shortly afterward she followed the others to the boat.

Merle had thought she wouldn't have the desire to come back once more later, alone, in the evening, after the grave was filled with sand and earth, but then she did it anyway.

She came alone. She hadn't even told Junipa what she had in mind, although her friend of course guessed. Probably they all knew.

"Hello, Merle," said Sekhmet, the Flowing Queen, perhaps the last of the old gods. She was waiting for Merle at the grave, a dark silhouette on four feet, very slender, very lithe. Almost unreal, had there not been the scent of wild animal wafting from the rock.

"I knew you would come here," said Merle. "Sooner or later."

The lion goddess nodded her furry head. Merle had trouble bringing the brown cat's eyes into harmony with that voice she'd heard inside for so long. But finally she managed to do it, and then she thought that really, they went quite well together. The same teasing, even contentious expression. But also eyes full of friendship and sympathy.

"There's no happy ending, is there?" Merle asked sadly.

"There never is. Only in fairy tales, but not even there particularly often. And if there is one, then it is usually made up." No question, it was the Flowing Queen speaking, no matter from what body and under what name.

"What happened?" asked Merle. "After you were yourself again, I mean."

"Did the others not tell you?"

Merle shook her head. "Junipa brought everyone through the mirrors to safety. You and your son . . . you were still fighting."

A breeze wafted over the nighttime desert and stirred the goddess's fur. Merle hadn't noticed the difference in the moonlight—everything here was gray, icy gray—but now she saw that Sekhmet's body was no longer of stone. Serafin's vital power had made her again what she had once been: an uncommonly slender, almost delicate lioness of flesh and blood and fur. She didn't look at all like a goddess. But perhaps that made her just that much more godly.

"We fought," said Sekhmet in a throaty voice. She sounded sad, probably not only for Serafin's sake. "Fought for a long, long time. And then I killed him."

"That's all?"

"What do details matter?"

"He was so big. And you are so small."

"I have eaten his heart."

"Well," said Merle, for nothing better occurred to her.

"The Son of the Mother," Sekhmet began, then she broke off and started over: "*My* son was perhaps big and very strong and even sharp—but he was never really a god. The sphinxes revered him as a god, and his magic was strong enough to bear their fortress through the mirror world. But he was eaten away by greed and hate and by a rage for which he had long forgotten the reason." She sadly shook her lion head. "I am not even sure whether he really recognized me. He had underestimated me. I opened his flank and ate through his entrails. Just like the time before." Sekhmet sighed as if what had happened made her sorry. "That time I left him his heart. This time not. He is dead and will remain so."

Merle let a moment pass before she asked, "And the sphinxes?"

"Those your friend has left alive are scattered to the winds. But there were not many. They have seen what I have done. And they fear me. I do not know what they will do. Hide, perhaps. A few will try to advance to the Stone Light, to their father. But they pose no more danger, not today."

"What happened to the Iron Eye?"

"Destroyed." Sekhmet noted the astonishment in Merle's face and purred gently. "Not by me. I guess it could not withstand the heat and cold that was called up inside it."

"Heat and cold," repeated Merle stupidly.

"Your two friends have not been idle."

"Winter and Summer?"

Sekhmet purred agreement. "They ground the mirrors between the elements. All that is left is a mountain of silver dust, which the Nile will carry away into the sea with the passage of time." She tilted her head toward the grave. "Do you want to see him? I can bring him here."

Merle thought about it for a couple of seconds, then shook her head. "I don't want anything more to do with all that."

"What do you plan to do now?"

Merle's eyes roamed over the insignificant grave mound once more. "Everyone is talking about the future. Eft is going to stay with the pirates"—she smiled fleetingly—"or with their captain, depending on whom one believes. So she can live in the sea, even if she isn't a mermaid anymore. And Dario, Aristide, and Tiziano . . . oh well, they want to become pirates too." Now she actually had to laugh. "Can you imagine that? Pirates! They're still only children!"

"You should be one too. At least a little."

Merle's eyes met the lion goddess's, and for a moment she felt in complete harmony with her, understood through and through. Perhaps they were still two parts of one and the same being, in some way; perhaps it would never really end, no matter what happened. "I haven't been a child since I . . ." Merle sought for the right words, but then she simply said, "Since the day I drank you."

Sekhmet gave out a lion sound that might have been laughter. "You actually believed that I would taste like raspberry juice!"

"You lied to me."

"Only fibbed."

"Fibbed *considerably*."

"A little."

Merle walked over to Sekhmet and put both arms around her furry lion neck. She felt the warm, rough lion tongue lick her behind the ear, full of tenderness and love.

"What are you going to do now?" Merle tried to suppress her tears, but she choked and the two of them had to laugh.

"Go north," said the lioness. "And then east."

"You want to find the Baba Yaga."

Sekhmet nodded on Merle's shoulder. "I want to know who she is. What she is. She has protected the Czarist kingdom all these years."

"As you did Venice."

"She had more success than I. Nevertheless, we could have much in common. And if not . . . well, it is at least *something* that I can do." Sekhmet again looked Merle in the eye. "But you have still not answered my question. What are you planning?"

"Junipa and I are going back to Venice. Eft and Calvino are taking us there. But we can't stay there long."

Sekhmet's eyes narrowed to tiny slits. "Junipa's heart."

"The Stone Light is too powerful. At least in this world."

"Then you will go with her? Through the mirrors?"

"I think so, yes."

The lion goddess licked her across the face, then she touched Merle's hand gently with the rough ball of one paw. "Farewell, Merle. Wherever you go."

"Farewell. And . . . I'm going to miss you. Even if you were a real pain in the neck."

The lioness purred softly at Merle's ear, then leaped over Serafin's grave in one spring, bowed in front of the dead boy under the sand, then turned and glided soundlessly into the night.

A gust of wind carried her scent back.

Vermithrax left the next morning.

"I'm going to look for my people, no matter what Seth said."

It pained Merle to see him go. It was the third departure in a few hours: first Serafin, then the Queen, now he. She didn't want him to leave her. Not him, too. But at the same time she knew that it didn't matter what she wished or did. Did not each of them seek a new task, a destiny?

"Somewhere they are living still," said Vermithrax. "Flying, talking lions like me. I know it. And I'll find them."

"In the south?"

"Rather in the south than elsewhere."

"Yes, I think that too," said Lalapeya, who was standing beside her daughter. "Perhaps they found protection there." Lalapeya wore her human form like a dress, Merle thought. Every time she saw her mother like that, it seemed to her a little like a masquerade. She was the most beautiful woman Merle knew, but still she was always a little more sphinx than human, even in that body. Merle wasn't certain if anyone else felt that.

She turned again to Vermithrax. "I wish you luck. And that we'll see each other again."

"We will." He bent forward and rubbed his huge nose on her forehead. For a moment she was blinded by the glow that he gave off.

Junipa walked up beside him and stroked his neck. "Good-bye, Vermithrax."

"I hope we'll meet again someday, little Junipa. And take care of your heart."

"I'll do that."

"And of Merle."

"Of her too." The two girls exchanged a look and smirked. Then they both fell on Vermithrax's neck together and only let him go when he growled "hey, hey" and shook as if he had fleas in his fur.

He turned around, unfolded his stone-feathered wings, and rose from the ground. His long tail whipped up sand. The ground was gradually drying out, now that the sun was in the heavens again.

They looked after him until he was only a glowing dot in the endless blue, a meteor in broad daylight.

"Do you think he'll really find them?" asked Junipa softly.

Merle didn't answer, only felt Lalapeya's bandaged hand on her shoulder, and then they went back to the boat together, where Eft was waiting for them.

The crew had polished the submarine to a high gloss. Golden pipes and door handles flashed; glass doors were, insofar as they were available, newly replaced; and a pirate who handled brush and paint better than a saber (Calvino said) had gone about repairing one of the ruined frescoes. Gradually he would take on the painting all over the boat. The captain had allowed him an extra ration of rum (for he painted better when he was drunk, he maintained), which made the other pirates offer themselves eagerly as helpers. Some had established a workshop, and every place in the boat was scrubbed, refined, and polished. Others discovered their cooking talents and prepared a festive meal in Merle's honor that wasn't bad at all. She was grateful and ate with appetite, but still, in her thoughts, she was somewhere else, with Serafin, who now lay alone on his rock and perhaps dreamed of the desert. Or of her.

Eft sat by Captain Calvino. Arcimboldo's mirror mask lay before her on the table. Sometimes, depending on how strongly the gas flames flickered in their little copper boxes and danced on the silver of Arcimboldo's cheeks, it looked as if his features were also moving, as if he were speaking or laughing.

Occasionally Eft bent forward and appeared to whisper something to him, but that might have been only an illusion and she was in truth reaching for a bowl or pouring wine into her goblet. But then what was it that made her break into laughter unexpectedly, even when neither Calvino nor one of the others had said anything? And why did she refuse to leave the mask below deck with the other treasures?

By the end of the meal she had wrung out of Calvino the promise to mount the silver face on the bridge, above the viewing window, where it could keep everything in view and, prophesied Calvino, probably know everything better than he. Eft stroked his hand and gave him a shark smile.

"All that's missing is for her to flutter her eyelashes at him," Junipa whispered in Merle's ear. The two burst out laughing immediately afterward when Eft gave the captain a flirtatious look that broke the rough fellow's resistance once and for all.

"I guess we don't need to worry about her anymore," said Merle, while Lalapeya, sitting with the two girls in her human form, laughed—in her, even that looked a little mysterious, like everything she did or said.

After the meal Junipa withdrew into the mirror world through a six-foot-tall mirror in her cabin. Only thus could she prevent the Stone Light gaining in power and influence over her. Of course she could have taken Merle and herself to Venice that way, but the two of them were enjoying the time left with Eft and the others. Furthermore, there was a promise that Merle intended to keep.

Somewhere in the Mediterranean, about halfway between continents, Calvino made the boat surface, in response to her request. Merle and her mother climbed out of the hatch onto the hull, walked over the tangle of splendid designs in gold and copper to the bow, and from there looked out over the endless sea. The surface nearby was moving, fish perhaps, or mermaids. They'd already met several. Now that the galleys of the Empire were floating rudderless on the sea, the sea women had come out of their hiding places and sank the warships wherever they encountered them.

Merle took the water mirror from Lalapeya. She touched the surface gently with her fingertips and said the magic word. The light vapor of the mirror phantom instantly gathered around her skin.

"I want to redeem my promise," she said.

The milky ring under her fingertips quivered. "Then the time has come?" asked the phantom.

"Yes."

"The sea?"

Merle nodded. "The biggest mirror in the world."

Lalapeya gently laid a bandaged hand on her shoulder. "You must give it to me."

Merle held her fingers in the interior of the oval frame a little longer. "Thank you," she said after she thought for a moment. "You probably don't know it, but without your help—"

"Yes, yes," said the phantom, "as if anyone had ever doubted it."

"You can't wait a moment longer, can you?"

"I can feel others. Others like me. The sea is full of them."

"Really?"

"Yes." He was sounding more and more excited. "They're everywhere."

"One more question."

"Umm."

"The world you came from . . . did it have a name?"

He thought it over for a moment. "A name? No. Everyone just called it 'the world.' Nobody knew there was more than one of them."

"That's exactly how it is here."

Behind them Calvino stuck his head out of the hatch. "Are you done yet?"

"Just a minute," Merle called back. Turning to the mirror, she said, "Good luck out there."

"You too."

She pulled her fingers out, and the phantom began to rotate, fast, like a whirlpool. Lalapeya received the mirror and closed her eyes. She raised the oval to her mouth and breathed on it. Then she murmured a string of words that Merle didn't understand. The sphinx opened her eyes and flung the mirror out into the sea. It flew through the air in a glittering arc. Shortly before impact, the water left the frame, an explosion of silvery beads, which melted into the waves immediately. The mirror splashed into the sea and went under.

"Is he—"

Lalapeya nodded at the waves, which thumped splashing against the hull. What Merle had taken at first for white foam revealed itself to be something nimble, ghostlike, that formed a multitude of crazy patterns before it looked like a hand waving good-bye and then faster than lightning whizzed away in a zigzag through the waves, away, away, away into freedom.

13

La Serenissima

Venice on a radiant morning, Venice liberated.

Seagulls screamed over the wrecks of galleys, half-sunk along the banks of the lagoon like the ribs of bizarre ocean creatures of wood and gold and iron. Men of the City Guard were posted on most of them to protect the wreckage from plunderers. Days would pass yet before the cleanup work in the city was far enough along for anyone to attend to the costly shipwrecks in the sea.

Above an island in the northeast of the lagoon, far away from the main island, a dark column stood out against the sky. Black smoke rose from the fires that burned there day and night. The fallen mummy soldiers were carried thither on ferries and laid on pyres for their final rest. The wind stood favorable and carried the ashes out over the sea.

Over the roofs and towers of the city the guardsmen flew their rounds on silent stone lions with widespread wings. The men were vigilantly observing the activities in the streets, making sure that no mummies lay undiscovered, even in the remotest back courtyards and gardens. Calling loudly from the sky, they directed the cleanup troops, repair crews, and soldiers on the ground. Down there all differences were suspended: Everyone, whether in uniform or day laborer, whether fisherman or tradesman, was busy cleaning up the streets, clearing the remains of mummy soldiers out of houses and from piazzas, and taking down the barricades, soot-blackened witnesses to the meager resistance against the Empire.

At the broad opening to the Grand Canal, Venice's main waterway, the activity was as lively as it used to be only on feast days. Dozens of boats and gondolas darted around on the water like ants at the foot of their hill, transports in one direction or the other. Everywhere, shouting and calling and sometimes even, again at last, individual songs from the sterns of polished gondolas.

On the bank of the canal mouth, at the harbor wall of the Zattere quay, stood Merle, Junipa, and Lalapeya. They waved at the departing rowboat that had brought them to shore. Tiziano and Aristide lay to the oars, while Dario and Eft waved good-bye with arms outstretched. The sea wind tore the words from their lips. The submarine lay far outside, on the other side of the ring of wrecked galleys, but none of the three turned away until the little dinghy was entirely out of sight. And even then they remained standing there, looking out over the water to where their friends had vanished.

"Will you go back with me for a little way?" Lalapeya asked finally.

Merle looked at Junipa. "How do you feel?"

The pale girl ran one hand over the scar on her chest and nodded. "Right now I don't feel anything. It's as if the Stone Light has withdrawn for the time being. Maybe to get over the defeat of the sphinxes."

Lalapeya, who had covered her petite woman's body with a sand-colored dress from the pirates' stores, led them through an alley deeper into the confusion of streets and piazzas. "The Light will probably rest for a while. After all, it has all the time in the world."

They crossed slender bridges, narrow courtyards, and the Grand Canal on a ferry. Merle was astonished at how fast the work of cleaning up was going. The traces of the thirty-year siege could not be removed within a few days, yet all the indications of the Empire's takeover of power were already erased from the cityscape. Merle wondered what had become of the Pharaoh's body. Probably they'd thrown it in the fire along with the mummies.

A young water carrier they met along the way told

them that the City Council had again taken over the business of governing. Many councillors had been executed by the Pharaoh, among them the traitors, and now their successors were trying to restore the credibility of the regime. It was said that they'd already gotten the advice of the Flowing Queen, who had returned to the lagoon with the downfall of the Empire; all decisions of the City Council would be hers; they would follow her will and would on no account anger her. Therefore it was in the population's interest to obey all orders and not to question the rule of the councillors. The young woman beamed with confidence. As long as the Flowing Queen watched over Venice, she was not afraid. She and the councillors would see to it that everything became good again.

Merle, Junipa, and Lalapeya nodded politely, thanked her for the information, and quickly went on their way to the sphinx's palazzo. No one had the heart to tell the young woman the truth about the Flowing Queen. And what sense would it have made? No one would have believed them. No one *wanted* to believe them.

In the palazzo they found many of the boys whom Serafin had excluded from the attack on the Pharaoh. They broke into shouts of joy when Lalapeya appeared in the doorway. She had no choice but to allow them to continue to live there—provided they made themselves useful working in the district and kept the salons and the corridors clean. Merle thought the company would be good for Lalapeya;

she would no longer feel so lonely in the big old building.

In the evening they sat together in the large salon and Merle and Junipa realized that this would be their last meal in this world for a long time. That made them sad and excited at the same time.

It had long been dark when Lalapeya led them into her chamber, through a labyrinth of silk curtains to a wall with a high mirror. The silver glass sparkled like the purest crystal. On the wooden frame were carved all the fabulous creatures of the Orient, a dance out of *A Thousand and One Nights*.

"Yet another good-bye," said Lalapeya, as the girls stood before her with bulging knapsacks filled with food and water canteens. "The last, I hope."

Merle was about to say something, but her mother gently laid a finger on her lips. "No," she whispered, shaking her head. "You know where you can find me whenever you want to. I will not leave here. I am the guardian of the lagoon. If the humans do not need me, perhaps the mermaids will."

Merle looked at her for a long moment. "It was you who built their cemetery, wasn't it?"

The sphinx nodded. "It lies under the palazzo. Someone must keep watch over it. And perhaps I can teach those boys out there that there is reason to respect the mermaids or even to be their friends. I think that would be a good beginning." She smiled. "Besides . . . it will soon be summer. Venice is wonderful when the sun is shining."

"Summer!" exclaimed Merle. "Of course! What became of her and Winter?"

"Became?" Lalapeya laughed. "Those two will never change. They go on through the world again as they have from the beginning of time, undisturbed by the fortunes of humans. And now and again they meet one another and then they act as if they were humans who are in love with each other."

"Aren't they, then?" Merle asked. "In love?"

"Perhaps they are. But perhaps there is no other choice for them. Not even they are entirely free."

Junipa kept thinking about what she'd said, but Lalapeya had already turned to Merle and put the question that had burned on her lips for too long. Merle had been waiting for it for days.

"You want to find him, don't you? Steven, I mean. Your father."

"Yes, perhaps," said Merle. "If he's still alive."

"Oh, that he certainly is," said the sphinx with conviction, "somewhere behind the mirrors. You've inherited your toughness and tenacity not just from me, Merle, but also from your father. Especially from him."

"We can look for him where we want to," said Junipa, and her mirror eyes seemed to blaze with determination. "In all worlds."

Lalapeya gently stroked Junipa's cheek with the back of her hand. "Yes, you can. You'll watch out for Merle, won't you? She broods too much when she's alone. She gets that from her mother."

"I won't be alone." Merle smiled at Junipa. "Neither of us will be." And then she hugged and kissed Lalapeya and finally took leave of her. Junipa touched the surface of the mirror and whispered the glass word.

Merle followed her through the wall of silver, out into the labyrinths of the mirror world, where there was so much to see, to learn, to find. Her father. That other Venice—that of the reflections on the canal. And even, who knew, another Merle, another Junipa.

Another Serafin.

But Lalapeya stood there for a long time after the two were gone and the mirror ripples had smoothed out. At last she turned around, parted the silken curtains with her bandaged hands, and strolled through the house, which was finally full of life again.

From far below, from the kitchen, it smelled of cinnamon and honey, and through the walls she could hear the ferment of the city, the awakening to the future. In between, so far away that no human ear could have perceived it, sounded the soft singing of the mermaids, somewhere in the sea, far away from all islands; behind it the call of the sea witch; the sprouting of a flower in desert sand; the wing beats of a powerful lion prince.

And perhaps even, very far away, very vague, the voices of two girls who had just walked out into another, alien world.